The Notorious Flynns Novellas

NO GENTLEMAN FOR GEORGINA
The Notorious Flynns Book 4

A MARQUIS FOR MARY
The Notorious Flynns Book 5

By

USA Today Bestselling Author
Jess Michaels

NO GENTLEMAN FOR GEORGINA
The Notorious Flynns Book 4

A MARQUIS FOR MARY
The Notorious Flynns Book 5

Copyright © Jesse Petersen, 2015

ISBN-13: 978-1512391794
ISBN-10: 1512391794

For more information, contact Jess Michaels
www.AuthorJessMichaels.com
PO Box 814, Cortaro, AZ 85652-0814

To contact the author:
Email: Jess@AuthorJessMichaels.com
Twitter www.twitter.com/JessMichaelsbks
Facebook: www.facebook.com/JessMichaelsBks

Jess Michaels raffles a FREE Kindle or Amazon gift certificate EVERY month to members of her newsletter, so sign up on her website:
http://www.authorjessmichaels.com/join-the-jess-michaels-newsletter/

Contents

No Gentleman for Georgina

(THE NOTORIOUS FLYNNS BOOK 4)

By

Jess Michaels

DEDICATION

For Grace Callaway, Delilah Marvelle, Heather Boyd, Vicki Lewis Thompson and all the other authors who looked me in the eye and said, "Leap!" Having you to keep me company as I built my wings has been fantastic.

And to Michael, master craftsman and repairer of wings. And holder of my heart while I tumble.

CHAPTER ONE

Paul Abbot had no idea why the Duke and Duchess of Hartholm insisted on inviting him to their balls and soirees. He had no title, little fortune and was nothing more than the manager at their brother-in-law's notorious club.

But perhaps that was the answer. His employer's new family, the Flynns, were welcoming to all comers, and for some reason he had been swept up in their wake. But he knew his place even if they pretended not to do the same.

And so he stood as far to the back of the ballroom as he could, watching the partygoers swirl by in their foppery and finery. He sipped his one and only drink for the evening and all but forced himself not to look at the pocket watch tucked in his jacket.

"Counting the moments until you can flee is not good manners," he murmured to himself as he stifled a yawn. There was nothing here to tempt him.

Nothing but…

The moment his mind began that errant thought, his gaze slid across the room and landed squarely on the one and only temptation London Society had ever held for him.

Miss Georgina Hickson stood on the other side of the room. And she was beautiful, just as she was always beautiful. Her dark blonde hair was fixed so that it framed her oval face perfectly, accentuating high cheekbones and full, rosy lips. He had wondered, more than once, how those lips would taste. Her bright blue eyes were expressive as she chatted with her companions.

Companions who were all men.

His heart sank. Georgina never seemed to be short of partners at the events they mutually attended. Paul held his breath every day when he looked at the notices in the Times, waiting to see an announcement of her impending nuptials to the Earl of Very Important Things or the Duke of So Far Above Paul Abbot.

As if she sensed his stare on her, she suddenly looked across the room. Her gaze locked on him and her smile broadened. His heart stuttered and he forced himself to smile back, to lift a hand in a polite wave.

She returned it, then spoke to her companions once more before she began to come across the room toward him.

Paul held his breath as he watched her approach. He had less than thirty seconds to give himself the same talk he always did when Georgina came near. The talk that reminded him that when they had been introduced at a party to celebrate the shocking marriage of his employer, Marcus Rivers, and Georgina's good friend Annabelle Flynn two years ago, that Georgina had only been polite to talk to him. That it was her continued politeness which drove her to carry on their odd friendship all these years later.

She was a nice girl and she had to recognize just how out of place he was at these gatherings. Beyond that, her interest in him was less than nothing.

"Mr. Abbot," she said, that beautifully melodious voice washing over him like a soothing rain after a too-hot day. "I did not know you were in attendance or I would have sought out your company sooner."

He swallowed hard and found his voice. "You seemed quite enthralled—I would not have pulled you away from your companions."

She glanced over her shoulder at her circle of men. "Them? Not enthralled, I assure you, nor they with me. We were discussing the weather, of all things." She rolled her eyes. "I cannot tell you how utterly uninterested I am in the Almanac's predictions for this year's rainfall."

He laughed. "That does sound rather dull."

"So in a way, you saved me," she said with another of those dazzling smiles. "I am most obliged."

"At your service," he said with a stiff bow that brought a twinge of pain to his shoulder. Pain he had been ignoring for well over a decade and intended to continue ignoring now.

"How are you, then?" she asked. "I feel like I have not seen you in an age. I always look forward to your company when I visit Annabelle and Marcus's home."

Paul shifted. He wished he could say the same to her, but from his lips those words would be a desperate confession versus her polite overstatement.

"With Rivers spending more time at home, we *do* often conduct our business there." He smiled.

"It must be rather thrilling, running such a successful establishment."

His smile slowly faded. Being an innocent, Georgina had no idea the truth about the club he managed. The Donville Masquerade, Rivers' den of sex and gambling, would horrify her if she ever did discover the reality of it.

"Sometimes I think I should sneak a visit there, perhaps convince Annabelle to allow it," she said with a light laugh.

Paul stiffened at the idea of Georgina there. Of watching her watch the debauched acts. Despite himself, his cock began to swell at the thought and he fought for the control he always held over himself before he said, "I doubt your father would approve of such a plan, Miss Hickson."

She shrugged, but the light in her eyes dimmed. "My father approves of so little I do anymore, Mr. Abbot. It makes me wonder if I should not try to please myself for a while since he will not be pleased by *any* action I do or do not take."

Paul took a step toward her even though it was improper to do so. He couldn't help it. Although Georgina rarely made comments like that one to him, he had watched her struggle with her family's increasing frustration at her lack of a marriage over the years. He wanted to comfort her somehow. Honestly, he wanted to know how the men of the *ton* had been so stupid as to not snatch her up already.

But before he could say anything, her face went pale and her eyes suddenly focused on a spot behind him.

"Georgina," came the sharp voice of none other than her father. Paul turned and gave a formal nod to the man, which was, as always, ignored. "Come, our presence is required elsewhere."

Georgina's lips pursed together, but she did not argue. She slowly moved away to her father's side. She turned back before they walked away. "Good evening, Mr. Abbot. I'm sorry we didn't get to speak further."

"Good night, Miss Hickson," he said as she began to disappear into the milling crowd once more.

The fact that she was lost to him within a moment of leaving his side was practically a metaphor, and he downed the rest of his drink in a swig.

"Don't be a fool," he muttered to himself as he set the empty glass aside to be collected by a servant at some point. "Whatever you wish would happen *never* will."

But even as he forced himself to move, find his hosts and excuse himself for the evening to get back to work, he realized that what he told himself would never change how he felt. It was impossible to change the desires that boiled inside of him. Desires that would remain forever unfulfilled.

Georgina winced as her father guided her into one of the Duke of Hartholm's private rooms and shut the door with a loud click. As he turned, she braced herself for the barrage of scolding bound to come, and he did not disappoint.

"What are you thinking?" he snapped.

She took a long breath. "About what, specifically?"

His eyebrows lifted. "No sass, now. You know what I'm talking about."

She turned her face, because, of course, she did know exactly what had upset her father this time. It was a subject that always caused consternation between them. Still, she shrugged. "I'm afraid I'm not certain what sin I have committed, Papa. You will have to clarify."

"Don't be daft," he said with a shake of his head. "We have talked about this many times. You had no reason to be standing in the middle of a crowded room with Paul Abbot."

Georgina walked away from him, wringing her hands. Her father had been haranguing her about Paul since the very first night she met him two years ago. He was not rich, and more importantly, he was not titled, so in her father's mind, there was no need for further discussion.

What he didn't know, what he didn't understand, was that in a room full of people Georgina had been fighting to impress for what would soon be four long Seasons, Paul never made her feel unworthy, or unwanted, or unpretty. When she talked to him, the time flew by. He was comfortable, he was wildly attractive, he was...he was...*Paul*. After she was with him, all she could think about were his soulful brown eyes, all she could wonder about was if his crisp, short brown hair was soft to the touch.

But she couldn't say that, for if her father knew the tender feelings the man inspired in her, he would likely forbid her not just from seeing him again, but from seeing Annabelle Rivers, Serafina Flynn, Gemma Flynn and Gemma's sister Mary, too. The Flynn wives and daughters had become the best friends she'd ever had.

"Mr. Abbot and I are friends, Papa," she said softly, hoping the gentling of her tone would lead to something similar in his.

Instead her father threw up his hands in something akin to

disgust. "The man's 'friendship' can do *nothing* for you. And perhaps if you were not so blasted distracted by this…this…bourgeois club manager, you would have earned your title last Season."

Georgina flinched. Her father hadn't always been so harsh with her. But the longer she remained on the marriage mart, the more intrusive and angry he became. She felt his disappointment and sometimes his disdain grow with each passing unsuccessful ball and soiree.

"I'm sorry I've let you down, Papa," she said softly.

He ignored her comment, or perhaps he had gotten so worked up, he didn't even hear it. "I will *not* see you destroy this new Season in the same way. You will not have many more chances, Georgina, and I tell you, you won't be wasting your time on unsuitable activities or men."

Georgina bit the inside of her mouth until she could taste blood. Oh, she talked a very brave game with Paul about doing what pleased her. And she had equally daring thoughts when it came to what she wanted. But she was too cowardly to actually follow through on any of that.

She pursed her lips and took a deep, cleansing breath before she said, "I promise you, Papa, I am as driven to succeed this year as you are."

And she was. To have been out for almost four years with no results wasn't only humiliating—it was exhausting. She had to be so perfect, so right, to follow so many rules. And the longer it went on, the more likely it became that she would be relegated to spinsterhood. A thought that gave her a shudder.

"I hope so," he said as he moved for the door. There he looked back at her. "I know I sound severe, but trust that I have your best interests at heart. I'll allow you a moment to gather yourself before you return to the ballroom."

He left her, and she sagged. In truth, she *did* think her father wanted the best for her. He was severe about it—he was sometimes very cold about it—but in his mind, he was trying to ensure her future.

Only the older she got, the longer she knew Paul and the more she saw her friends marrying men they truly loved, the more she had begun to question the future her father foresaw for her.

But there were things no one could ever change. She was foolish to hope for more when it was very likely more would never come.

CHAPTER TWO

Georgina looked up from the paper and could hardly contain her excitement. "Papa, did you read the news?"

Her mother and father had been talking, but now both shifted their attention to her. "What news?" her mother asked.

"Madame Tussaud's traveling wax exhibit is back in London after years touring the countryside," she said, turning the paper so they could see the advertisement. "I hadn't realized it returned a few months ago, but with everyone coming to Town for the Season, they're doing a special showing with new figures."

Her mother's eyes, dark blue like her own, suddenly filled with worry, and her father's face drew down with a frown.

Georgina rushed to avoid the refusals that were clearly on their lips, hoping she could find a way to convince them. "I've always wanted to see the figures," she said. "You know that many very important people have posed for Madame. Even the titled."

Her mother shot a side glance at her father before she answered Georgina. "I think I recall you asking to see the exhibit when it first came to London. You were less than ten, and of course we couldn't allow it."

Her father snorted out a derisive laugh. "Just as we won't allow it now, Eugenia."

Georgina sucked in a breath. "Oh, Papa! You know her

figures are all the rage."

His eyes narrowed. "Many things are the 'rage', Georgina. Many very inappropriate things that could damage you."

"Papa, I'm not asking if I may ride astride in Hyde Park," she argued. "This is art! No one could think that it would be inappropriate to—"

"The very idea of it is garish and disgusting," her father interrupted with a wave of his hand. "It is one thing to go look at a pretty portrait in the gallery or to learn needlepoint, but to take death masks of those who were killed in the Revolution? Or to mold a woman's body out of wax and dress it up? That is *not* art, Georgina. And I shall not have my daughter taking any part in it."

Georgina pushed the paper aside, frustration mounting in her. Hadn't she done everything her father had asked of her over the years? Hadn't she primped and prepared and said yes when she meant no and danced with men with bad breath only because someone called them "my lord"? Why couldn't he allow her this one pleasure?

"Papa," she began. "Please, you must listen to me—"

"I said no and that is the end of it," he said, slapping a hand down on the table.

She turned to her mother, hoping to find an ally, but she merely shook her head gently and Georgina slumped in her chair. It seemed she was destined to be stuck in the life her parents designed for her. There would not even be release for a little diversion like seeing the wax exhibit.

She took the section of the paper with the advertisement for Madame Tussaud's exhibit and quietly excused herself from the table. And tried very hard, as she trod up the stairs to her chamber, not to cry with disappointment that seemed to mount each day.

Paul sat at the desk in Marcus's study, looking over paperwork his employer had asked him to review that afternoon. They had once held these meetings in the office above the main room of the hell Marcus owned, but in the two years since Marcus's marriage to Annabelle, Paul had found himself in their home more and more. And there he was witness to the loving bond that was shared between husband and wife.

On one hand, he was truly happy for his friend. Marcus had helped him in ways the other man probably didn't even realize, and seeing him content as he was pleased Paul. But it was also a form of torture. Marcus and Annabelle's sideways stares and lingering touches only illustrated just how alone in the world Paul was.

He shook his head and pushed the chair away from the desk. He was being maudlin, something that was bound to happen when he spent too much time poring over figures. And since Marcus had slipped from the room half an hour before, Paul hadn't even had someone to talk to in the hopes he could clear his mind.

He moved to the sideboard to pour himself tea, but as he neared the door, he heard voices in the hallway. Female voices, lifting and falling as if there was an argument happening. Curious and needing to stretch his legs, he stepped into the hallway and came to a short stop as he found Annabelle standing in the foyer with Georgina.

The women were so involved in talk that for a moment they didn't notice him. He couldn't make out exactly what they were saying, but Georgina was speaking rapidly, her face and tone revealing her upset, and she was waving around what looked like a piece of newspaper.

He should have simply turned around and walked back to the study to complete his work. But seeing Georgina here was too strong a draw. He found himself walking toward the women, his legs moving almost without his permission.

As he entered the foyer, he heard Annabelle say in a

soothing tone, "Dearest, please, you are making no sense at all. You must calm yourself and come with me. We'll sit down and have tea and work out whatever is wrong—"

At that moment, he cleared his throat and both women jumped as they realized his presence. Georgina's face went bright red and she shoved the torn paper in her hands down into the reticule dangling from her wrist.

"Oh, Paul," Annabelle said with a smile. "I'm sorry, we didn't see you there. You remember Georgina, of course."

Georgina still did not look at him even as he bowed slightly. "Miss Hickson. I'm sorry to disturb you. I was merely stretching my legs and I heard voices. I don't wish to interrupt."

Georgina looked at him at last. "You aren't, of course, Mr. Abbot. I didn't know you were here."

Annabelle gave her an odd look. "If you and Marcus are taking a break from your work, perhaps you will join Georgina and me for tea?"

Paul continued to look at Georgina, wishing he could comfort her in some way even though he didn't know why she was so upset. "I'm afraid I don't know where Marcus went. He made some reference to an errand a short while ago and left me to my own devices."

Annabelle blinked. "An errand, was it? Interesting. Well, come and join us regardless."

He knew he should decline, especially since Georgina obviously had something private to discuss with Annabelle, but the opportunity to sit with her without her mother and father clucking their tongues in disapproval was too rare to pass up.

"I will come in for a while, thank you," he said.

"Excellent," Annabelle said as she linked arms with Georgina and led them both into the parlor.

As she rang the bell, Paul watched Georgina pace across the room to the window that overlooked the garden. Her expression was pensive and sad as she stared out over beautiful flowers and well-manicured bushes.

"Miss Hickson—" he began, but was stopped when a servant entered with refreshments. The young woman set her tray down, then leaned in to say something to Annabelle. The other woman blushed, but smiled as she looked toward her friend and Paul.

"Won't you excuse me a moment? Marcus has requested my company."

The light in her eyes made Paul turn his head. So *that* was the something Marcus had left him for. Some surprise for Annabelle.

"Of course," Georgina said, her tone flat as she turned to face her friend. "I will be fine alone if Mr. Abbot has his work to attend to."

Annabelle waved her hand. "Don't be silly. I'm certain he will be happy to keep you company." She smiled at Georgina. "I won't be long. I promise."

Georgina nodded and Annabelle left, leaving the door just slightly ajar for propriety. Paul stared at it. He had never been so alone with Georgina before. He had always spent his time with her in ballrooms and parlors filled with people.

She shifted, and her awkward smile told him she was thinking the same thing. But was she uncomfortable with their state of privacy? Was that why she had said she would be fine alone?

"You must not have thought you would be relegated to governess duty today," she finally said, moving toward him.

He shook his head. "What?"

She blushed. "You came here to work, not be forced to keep my company. I know you were only being polite not telling Annabelle you wished to leave."

He took a small step toward her. "Actually, I do not mind spending time with you at all, Miss Hickson," he said softly. "It is always a pleasure. But if you'd like me to leave—"

"No!" she said, the sudden and strong tone of her denial making him smile wider. Her cheeks grew even darker. "I mean, I would certainly enjoy your company."

He motioned her to the settee and then poured her tea. After years of watching her, he knew how she took it, so he prepared it and handed it over. She took a sip and looked up at him in surprise.

"Th-thank you," she stammered.

He poured his own refreshment and sat down across from her. "I have not seen you since Lord and Lady Hartholm's soiree a few days ago."

She nodded. "Yes. I was sorry you left before I could say goodbye."

He shrugged. "I am not particularly comfortable at such events, I fear. It is not my world."

She shifted. "Perhaps not, but that does not mean you are not welcome there. I know many a lady watches you at those events, wishing you would dance with them."

He drew back in surprise at that statement. "You must be joking."

"No." She dropped her gaze. "I am asked about you on a regular basis. Because we are...we are friends of a sort."

He nodded. Friends. He was lucky to be able to call her that. And yet sitting here, looking at her, knowing she was hurting and it was not his place to help her...he wanted so much more.

"How much did you hear between Annabelle and me in the hall?" she asked.

He was caught off guard by the soft question. "Not much," he admitted. "Enough to know you have been distressed by something. Perhaps whatever was in the newspaper you tried to hide when you saw me in the foyer."

She looked down at her clenched hands in her lap for a moment, and he could see the struggle on her face. She obviously wanted to talk to someone about her troubles, and with Annabelle out of the room, here he was. He shouldn't have allowed that, knowing it was inappropriate for her.

But he didn't care.

"If you would like to share what has happened with me, I

promise not to judge you."

Her gaze jerked up and she met his eyes. Her stare was so deep and blue and beautiful that he couldn't tear himself away. She held there for a short time before she removed her reticule from her wrist and withdrew from it that crumpled piece of newspaper.

He took her offering and smoothed the wrinkled paper out. He scanned the words, looking for whatever could have bothered her. When he was silent too long, she whispered, "The advertisement."

His gaze fell on the small square in the corner that touted a return of Madame Tussaud's wax figures to London.

"The exhibit?" he asked, looking up.

She nodded. "That is what I came to talk to Annabelle about, though I hadn't yet explained it. You must think me very silly."

He furrowed his brow, still uncertain why this would cause her such strong emotion. "Not at all," he said as he handed the paper back. "It's a wonderful exhibit—you will enjoy it, I'm certain."

Her face fell and she reached out to rest her fingers on the paper she had placed beside her on the settee. "No, I will not," she said, her voice barely carrying. "My father won't allow me to attend."

He drew back as the pain in her voice became clear. "Why not?"

She looked at him for a very long time. Long enough that he wondered if she intended to answer the question at any point. "My father has a certain desire for my future. And he will refuse me the right to anything that isn't in his plans for me."

Paul couldn't stop his frown from deepening. "And so he will eliminate any pleasure from your life?"

The moment he asked the question, he heard the double entendre to it. One he hadn't meant but which now sent his errant mind on a journey of kissing this woman. Undressing her. Making love to her.

She blushed. "He feels the exhibit is inappropriate. Even if it is all the rage to see it."

"That is patently unfair, to deny you what you desire. If he didn't want to attend, why not allow you another chaperone?"

She shrugged. "As I said, it is outside the bounds of his plans for me. So it will not happen." She looked at him for a moment. "You appear very upset on my behalf, which I appreciate. But do not worry yourself. I only wanted to tell someone about my disappointment. I have never thought for a moment that this problem could be fixed by anyone. I won't be allowed to go and that is the end of it."

Paul pressed his lips together in displeasure. Georgina was so resigned to whatever her parents desired. So surrendered to a life she would have at their behest. He knew he could not change that life, that future, but suddenly he very much wanted to give her this small boon.

"I..." He shook his head, almost in disbelief at himself that he would say this. "What if I could help you?"

CHAPTER THREE

Georgina blinked in confusion as she stared at Paul. He didn't look like he was making fun of her, but if he wasn't teasing, she was truly flummoxed by what he could mean.

"Help me?" she repeated. "Help me what?"

He swallowed before he spoke. "I could help you see the exhibit."

She pushed to her feet and took a long step toward him. Suddenly they were too much in each other's space. She'd never been so close in all the times they met, for they had never danced. He was very tall indeed, very handsome, and he smelled spicy and sinful. She tried hard to draw breath, to sound calm even when her racing heart betrayed her to herself.

"You would do that?" she asked, the words broken.

He nodded slowly. "Yes. If you desired me to do so."

"Why?" she asked, then immediately regretted it. There were more answers to the question that would break her heart than ones that would make her soul soar.

He hesitated a moment, as if trying to formulate the proper response. Then he shrugged ever so slightly. "Because I like you, Georgina Hickson. I think you deserve to see the exhibit. You deserve *something* you want."

She stopped breathing entirely. Those words were not the ones she had expected. And he had called her Georgina. Well, he'd called her by her full name, so that wasn't quite as intimate, but it was certainly more so than referring to her formally and properly as he had done since the first moment they met.

"I want—" she began, then turned away. Great God, she hadn't actually been about to admit what she truly wanted, had she? There would be nothing so foolish, since it was not a feeling he likely returned, nor could it ever amount to anything.

"What do you want?" he said from behind her, his voice suddenly rough.

She swallowed hard and faced him, forcing herself to maintain some kind of nonchalance. "How would we do it?"

He pondered that. "Your father allows you to spend the night here from time to time, does he not?"

Georgina paused. "Sometimes. Begrudgingly."

"Arrange it with Annabelle, and I will be certain the back servants' entrance is left open. You can sneak out once the household is abed and I'll meet you behind the house. Afterward I will bring you back. No one will ever be the wiser."

She shivered as the delicious wrongness of that plan sunk in. It would flout propriety of all kinds. "In the middle of the night," she repeated.

He nodded. "That would be for the best. It will ensure you'll not be seen and no one will know who might report back to your father."

"And how will we manage to get in?" she asked. "I would imagine that the Magnificent Mercatura will be locked tight at two in the morning."

He smiled, but it was a different expression than any of the ones she'd ever seen him flash before. There was a smug maleness to it, a confidence that made a queer ache begin in the pit of her stomach. Warmth seemed to spread through her, pooling in the most inappropriate places.

"Rivers is a very influential man," he drawled. "And so am I. The proprietress of the exhibit...well, she has been known to frequent the club. I think she would allow it if she understood how good a cause it is."

She blinked. She knew very little about Marcus Rivers' club. It was a scandalous place, the Donville Masquerade, but everyone always stopped talking about it when she entered the room. When she'd asked Annabelle about it directly, her friend had actually blushed to the roots of her hair and muttered something about changing the subject.

Which only left her desperately curious about what it was exactly that Paul did.

She pushed those thoughts aside as he tilted his head, watching her too closely. Seeing too much.

"Will you?" he asked.

Doing this would be dangerous, and she knew it. But she couldn't resist and not just because she wanted to see the wax figures. Slowly, she nodded. "When?"

His face relaxed, as if he had been nervous about her answer. "I'll need at least three days to arrange it. What about Thursday night?"

"Very well. If I cannot get my father's permission to stay here, I'll send word through Annabelle. If you hear nothing, assume it will happen."

He nodded, his eyes lingering on her face for far too long. Then he shook his head as if shaking off a spell and said, "Good. Very good. And now I *should* probably return to my work."

She watched him as he turned away toward the door. But before he took a step, he turned back. "Georgina?"

She jolted. Now he truly was saying her first name. It was utterly inappropriate to do so, and yet it made her entire body flutter with nothing short of desire.

"Y-Yes?"

He seemed to struggle for a moment, but then he said, "Goodbye."

"Goodbye, Pa—Mr. Abbot," she whispered, not bold enough to call him by his first name. "I will see you soon, I hope."

He slipped from the room and she all but collapsed on the settee closest to her. When she was with him, he always seemed to hold sway on all the air in the room, but never more than today when he proposed such a wild plan to her. And she had accepted!

Normally she wasn't so brave, but to have him hold her gaze as he had, to have him whisper that she deserved something for her own pleasure...how could she refuse? She would get time alone with him. And she would get to the see the wax exhibit.

There could be nothing more perfect.

Her reverie was interrupted when Annabelle returned to the room. Her face was flushed and her hair slightly askew. She smoothed it as she walked toward Georgina.

"Is everything all right? You are very pale."

Georgina jumped. She was not going to tell Annabelle about her odd plan with Paul. If she said it out loud, it might make it not real. Or her friend might discourage her.

"I am fine," she insisted with a bright smile she did not have to fake.

Annabelle arched a brow. "Yes, you do seem in higher spirits than you did when you arrived. But where is Abbot?"

Georgina pushed to her feet and poured herself another cup of tea. "He had to return to his work."

"I hope you weren't alone long," Annabelle said.

She faced her friend. "Not at all. I had time to think."

"Do you want to tell me what was upsetting you so much upon your arrival?" Annabelle asked, watching Georgina far too closely. "You were waving around the paper and so incoherent that I didn't understand."

Georgina shook off her friend's concern. "You know, I find I am less upset now than I was. It is truly not worth discussing."

Annabelle drew back. "You came all the way here and were ranting in my foyer, but now it is not worth discussing?"

"Oh, it was just my father, trying to control my future

again," Georgina explained. "But it matters very little now, I assure you."

"Georgina…" Annabelle began, her tone concerned.

"Do you think I might be able to spend the night here on Thursday?" Georgina interrupted.

Annabelle tilted her head slightly and then nodded. "Er, of course. You are always welcome here, you know that is true."

Georgina smiled at her friend, but she was utterly distracted. All she could think about was Paul's offer to take her to the exhibit. Paul's handsome face. Paul in general.

"What is going on with you?" Annabelle asked, her sharp tone breaking into Georgina's thoughts.

She gathered up her reticule with a smile. "Nothing at all. I'll send word about what time I'll join you as soon as I get permission from my father, if that is amenable to you."

Annabelle took a step forward and her hand closed around Georgina's gently. "Georgina."

She nodded. "Yes?"

"I know it is difficult for you right now," her friend said gently. "What your father wants…it is a great deal of pressure on you. I also realize he disapproves of our friendship, but I want you to know how much I value it."

Thoughts of Paul fled as Georgina met her friend's bright eyes. Annabelle seemed truly concerned about her, and it was the reason she loved the other woman so much. In a world where everyone had their ulterior motives about her, Annabelle seemed to truly love her just for who she was.

"As do I," she whispered, blinking at the tears that had suddenly flooded her eyes. "More than you likely know."

Annabelle's eyes also sparkled with unshed tears. "Then are you certain there is nothing you wish to tell me? You know I would be happy to help or support you in any way."

Georgina hesitated. She had never spoken to her friend about her feelings for Paul. She doubted Annabelle even suspected the truth. And there was part of her that longed to whisper what she had held inside for almost two years. But another part didn't want to open that door.

Annabelle would want to protect her, of that Georgina was certain. And if her friend told her not to meet with Paul...or worse yet told her that Paul could never care for her...

Well, she wanted to live in her fantasy, at least for a while longer. It had been so long since she had something to look forward to. She didn't want to lose it.

"No, nothing at all," she reassured Annabelle. Then she squeezed her friend's hand. "And I should go. My father is already in a bit of a dudgeon, so I probably shouldn't have left this afternoon."

Annabelle caught her breath, as if to speak, but then shook her head. "Well, perhaps you will want to speak more on Thursday. We look forward to having you."

Georgina smiled, then led her from the room to call for her carriage. But as it pulled up and she said her goodbyes, she couldn't help all but dancing from the house. She was going to have an evening with Paul.

And even though it could mean nothing, at that moment it meant everything in the world.

CHAPTER FOUR

Paul sat in the narrow alleyway behind Rivers' home on Thursday night in one of his employer's fine rigs. Marcus always allowed Paul to borrow them and had asked no question when he asked for the privilege that night. In fact, Marcus had teased him, prodding him about if he had perhaps found something to do with a woman.

If only his friend knew the truth. Paul could already hear Marcus's voice ringing in his ears, lecturing him about how out of reach Georgina was and telling him to walk away. He pushed it aside, along with his own misgivings and stared, unblinking, at the servants' entrance. Within a moment or two, the door slowly opened.

He straightened and caught his breath as Georgina slipped into the darkness of the night. She was dressed as though she were going to a ball, in fine pale blue silk with her hair done perfectly. He stepped down from the phaeton and moved on her.

She smiled through the dim moonlight. "I'm so glad you're here. I feared you might have changed your mind."

"I would not," he said softly, though in truth he had reconsidered this course of action dozens of times in the past few days. Everything in him knew this was a mistake and yet he was making it regardless.

Seeing Georgina look up at him in excitement and

pleasure was well worth it.

"Shall we go?" he asked, motioning to Marcus's rig.

She nodded and took his hand for help up into the phaeton. As he touched her, a spark seemed to jolt through him. By God, but he wanted her. But he frowned for he knew that would never be.

He joined her and flicked the reins so the horses would move, and they eased onto the street. It was late, so the roads were mostly quiet. Their only companions were the occasional rig bringing home revelers.

They rode in silence for a bit, but then Paul sent her a look from the corner of his eye. "You look beautiful, Miss Hickson. Does that mean you had your maid help you? Can you trust her?"

Georgina glanced over at him. "I do not think I could trust Molly, in truth. She would likely rush to tell my father all my sins if she knew about tonight. No, I prepared myself, Mr. Abbot." He drew back in surprise and she laughed. "We ladies of the *ton* are not all so useless as you seem to think. And this dress fastens along the front, so that did make it easier to help myself."

He stifled a groan at the thought of Georgina fastening her dress. Of unfastening it and revealing all the creamy skin beneath.

"Are you all right?" she asked. "You made a very funny noise just then."

He nodded. "Very well, thank you."

"I want to thank you again for arranging for this," Georgina said, clasping her hands before her. "You have no idea how I have been dancing around the house, looking forward to this night. At supper tonight, even Marcus and Annabelle commented on how I looked happier than I have in years. And it is all thanks to you, Paul. I mean, Mr. Abbot."

Paul stiffened at the sound of his name coming from her pink lips. As he turned the phaeton up a side street, he considered his options. Tonight was a stolen moment out of

23

time, after all. Should he not take advantage?

"You should call me by my first name if it pleases you," he said. "We are not in company, after all."

She seemed to ponder that for a moment. "Very well, Paul. And you will call me Georgina, I hope. Miss Hickson has always seemed too formal to me."

He squeezed his eyes shut for a brief second. God, calling her Georgina was an exercise in pain. He wanted to whisper that name. Moan it. Taste it on his tongue even as he tasted her.

This was most definitely a terrible mistake.

They turned down the last street, and there was the Magnificent Mercura waiting for them at the end of the lane. Of course, at night, with its lamps extinguished and the streets empty, it looked far from Magnificent. It was just another drab building along the road, surrounded by other equally nondescript shops.

"We will go around the back," he explained as he guided the phaeton into the alleyway, "and the servant will let us in."

Georgina's blush was obvious even in just the dim streetlamps. "Will—will this person recognize me?"

He pulled the rig to a stop behind the building and turned to look at her full on. "I very much doubt it. After all, this is the servant of a woman who is treated as little more than a merchant in this country. If you walked into a store in Cheapside, someplace far from where you live, would you expect the shopkeep to know you?"

She shook her head. "No, my family is certainly not so well-known that would happen. Perhaps they might know my uncle, the marquis, but even that would be questionable."

He nodded. "So you see, there is nothing to fear. And even if there was, I explained to Madame Tussaud—"

Her eyes lit up. "You spoke to her?"

He laughed at the thrill in her tone. "I did, Georgina. As I said, she sometimes frequents the Donville Masquerade. I explained to her some of the circumstances—without naming names—and she assured me she would send only her most discreet man to welcome us. He'll let us in and then all but vanish until we leave and he locks the place back up. So you have nothing to fear."

She smiled, her gaze lingering on him. "When it comes to you, it seems that is very true. You think of everything."

He cleared his throat, uncomfortable with her rapt attention when he knew her feelings didn't match his own. Without another word, he climbed down from the rig and around to her side where he took her hand and helped her from the high phaeton.

He was about to release her hand, free himself from the heat and electricity that shot through him when he dared touch her, but she wouldn't allow it. She grasped his hand with both hers and drew him closer.

"I know I said it once, but I'll say it again before we start. Thank you, Paul. Thank you so much."

He wanted to kiss her. A desperate, powerful desire that nearly overtook his reason as he stood staring down at her in the dark. He snatched his hand away and turned toward the door.

"You're welcome," he muttered while he knocked.

She said nothing as they waited for the servant, but the uncomfortable silence didn't linger long. The door opened and a squat little man awaited them with a lantern in his hand.

"You Abbot?" he asked, peering past Paul to Georgina.

Paul nodded. "Indeed, I am. Are you Winston?"

"Come in, come in. The treasures await you," he said, his voice suddenly taking on a jolly, barker quality.

Paul stepped aside and motioned for Georgina to go first. She kept her eyes averted from him as she did so. He could see his abruptness had hurt her feelings. But of course, had he followed through on his unforgivable desire to kiss her...well, she would have been more than just put out. She probably would have smacked him and run screaming into the dark to escape his unwanted advances.

They followed Winston down a series of back hallways

until he stopped at a tall door. He handed over the lantern to Paul with a smile.

"Through here is the main foyer and where you will begin your tour," he said. "I lit a few lamps here and there, but not many of them so we won't attract interest from the street, you see. You'll need to use the lantern to guide your way. Oh, but don't lean it too close. Wouldn't want to melt away some lord or lady's face, would we?"

He burst into a throaty, smoky laugh that brought smile to Georgina's face.

"No, that would be terrible," she agreed, some of the humor back in her voice. "Will you be all right guiding yourself through the dark back here, Mr. Winston?"

He chuckled again. "Me? I know these passages like the back of my hand, but thank you for your concern, miss. When you're ready to leave, snuff out the candle by the main entrance. I can see that light from Madame's office and I'll know you're ready to leave so I can guide you out through the maze. Enjoy yourselves."

He gave a tiny bow, clearly meant for her, and then scuttled away back into the dark, leaving Paul and Georgina alone. Paul smiled at her, hoping to reassure her after he'd hurt her feelings. "Are you ready?"

Her grin was back, lighting up her already pretty face, but giving it more joy and animation. "I am so very, very ready!"

He waited no more, but opened the secret side door into the foyer. He allowed her to enter first, holding the lantern high as she slipped past him, leaving a trail of soft, sweet scent in her wake. Paul drew a deep breath of it before he followed her in.

She came to a stone stop, her hands clasped at her breast as she stared around the first room. There were only a few figures here, but Georgina stared at them with a focused attention and wonderment that Paul could not help but smile over. She was so utterly enchanted and enchanting.

And in that moment, he had never been happier that he

had broken out of the normal regime of his life and taken her here. Even if it *was* only a stolen moment in time, he would take it and savor it and live it over and over later.

Georgina could scarcely breathe as she stepped up to yet another fine figure that Madame Tussaud had labored over. Paul stood behind her, holding up the lantern for her, just as he had been with all the figures in the foyer and into this second display room.

"How can they be so lifelike?" she whispered as she reached her hand out. But she stopped before she could touch, unwilling to ruin the artwork with her fingers.

"Years, decades of practice in her art," Paul said softly. "She made the death masks from the Revolution, you know."

She nodded. "I read that somewhere. What a sad and beautiful duty to perform, capturing the last moment of someone's life, especially after such a violent end. It must have been horrible for her."

Paul said nothing, and even though Georgina continued to stare at the figure before her, she winced slightly. He must think her very silly if the way he jerked away from her earlier or how he grew silent when she prattled on were any indications.

She stepped forward in the room. At the end were two signs, one pointing right, the other left.

"If we go right, we can see those famous death masks," she said. "Left takes us to the East India Company. Which would you prefer?"

She turned to receive his answer, but found Paul standing stock still, the lantern in his hand trembling ever so slightly as he stared at the sign she had just read. He said nothing, but slowly turned to the left and walked away.

She followed him, confused by the sudden change in his

expression, his demeanor.

"Mr. Abbot?" she asked as he stopped in front of a tableau of several East India Company troops. He said nothing. "Paul?" she asked, this time softer.

His hand continued to shake as he lifted the lantern and leaned in to the figures. His face was very pale and his eyes spoke of a sadness, a depth of loss that made Georgina's chest hurt as she stared at him.

Perhaps she should have stepped away, left him to ponder these figures alone. But there was something in her that would not allow that. Instead, she leaned forward and touched his forearm.

"Paul, what is it? What troubles you so?"

He jolted a bit at the contact and turned his face to look at her. There was a hollow quality to his eyes that even in the dim light was obviously caused by some deep pain.

"I'm sorry," he murmured, moving to turn away.

She could have let him go, but she didn't. "Please," she whispered. "You are obviously upset by this exhibit. Won't you tell me why?"

He seemed to struggle with that question for a long moment, then he nodded. "Very well. I-I'm sure you don't know, but I once served with the East India Company."

She drew back. "You did? Marcus has never said anything about it."

"He may not know, we have never spoken about it," Paul said with a shrug. "I joined when I was but sixteen. It was a way to escape the life I was born into." He looked at her for a long time. "You wouldn't understand."

She flinched. "Perhaps not the circumstances, as I suppose you believe I have never encountered hardship. But as far as wishing to escape the life I was born into, I believe I understand that somewhat. But to be so young…"

"I was not the youngest, I assure you. At first, it was all fun and adventure. Oh, it was blasted hot, of course, and sometimes unpleasant, but mostly I loved every moment. Then there was a cholera outbreak and we lost sixty percent of our group."

"Oh, Paul."

"I watched men die terrible deaths. I waited to be stricken, and I was. But I survived." He shook his head. "The year I turned twenty I was shot during a skirmish to gain control over a little corner of land that would make a trade route easier."

"Paul!" she gasped, her grip on his arm tightening out of reflex. "How badly were you hurt?"

"I nearly lost my arm," he admitted, his tone dull. "And I was sent back to London where I had nothing. For a year I drank and lost myself and suffered the pain of the injury. But then I met Marcus, and here we are. But looking at these uniforms..." He shook his head as he turned away. "It is like going back in time."

She stepped in front of him, watching his face. She had never seen him like this, so open, so emotional. Normally, he kept himself in the deepest, most severe check, never allowing emotion to bleed through. But he could not cover the pain of his memories now.

She lifted her hand and gently cupped his cheek, stroking her fingers over the skin.

"I cannot imagine what it must have been like. Did you have no one to talk to about it?"

He was staring at her now, his focus shifted from the past to her face. And a new expression joined whatever pain he had shown her. But she couldn't name it. All she could see was that it was hot and focused and made her stomach flip in a most pleasant fashion.

"No," he whispered. "No one knows what happened to me. You are the first soul I have ever spoken to."

"And your arm?"

"My shoulder still hurts from time to time." He rotated it with a slight wince. "But I am a whole man, if that is what you are asking me."

She swallowed. There was such a tension between them

now that she could hardly breathe. Hardly think. Instead, she whispered, "Paul…"

He let out a low moan and moved even closer to her. They were almost touching now, she was almost in his arms.

"Say my name again and I may not be able to stop myself," he whispered, his voice painfully rough.

She blinked, not understanding, and yet her body reacting in ways she did not control. She felt hot, so hot, and she was trembling as she slowly wet her dry lips and said, "Stop yourself from what?"

He leaned away, watching her face with an intensity that made her shake. "Georgina," he whispered. "You must know that I have—I have feelings for you."

CHAPTER FIVE

The moment those horrible words of confession fell from his lips, Paul wished he could take them back. Especially when Georgina's expression twisted into one of utter shock. He had gone too far, let his emotional response to the East India Company figures and the memories they inspired make him lose his faculties.

Georgina was kind to him, but there was nothing more there. And now he had ruined everything between them.

"Georgina," he began, intent on apology and minimization of this foolish mistake.

But before he could continue, she shocked him by launching herself forward into his arms. Her hands cupped his cheeks, and she kissed him.

For a fraction of a moment, he could only register surprise. Georgina was a proper lady in all things—and this reaction was anything but proper. But that surprise faded at the innocent ardor of her kiss, and he couldn't resist what she offered.

His arms came around her. He cupped the back of her head gently, angling her for better access, and returned the kiss. At first it was chaste and closed-mouthed, but her lips were too soft, her breath too sweet, and he couldn't help himself. He had to taste her.

He darted his tongue out, tracing the crease of her lips. When she gasped, he took the opportunity and slid inside. She stiffened only for a flash and then relaxed, first letting him slide his tongue over hers, then tentatively returning the passion in his kiss.

She was so innocent and yet she learned quickly, and soon she was delving into exploration with as much fervor as he felt. And it was too much temptation, too much desire that she stoked in him. He felt his cock beginning to swell, his blood beginning to boil, everything in his mind and body demanding that he strip her propriety away and claim her in some way.

He couldn't claim. That would be desperately unfair to her. But couldn't he give pleasure? Couldn't he have that small boon to cling to later when Georgina had married some proper man and she would likely not even be allowed to call him friend? That time was coming, he knew it, and he wanted this stolen night to give him comfort when it was all over.

He slowly guided her back, toward an exhibit where an elegantly dressed wax figure stood beside a velvet settee. When he lowered her to the seat, she didn't resist. Her kiss didn't slow, she didn't pull away. In fact, she let out a low, needy moan that made his cock even harder.

He knelt beside her as she reclined and slowly let one hand roam down her collarbones, her chest, until he gently cupped her left breast. When he did so, Georgina gasped and finally broke their kiss. She looked up at him in the dim light, her eyes wild and filled with both confusion and need.

"Paul?" she whispered, her voice harsh and broken.

He stared into her eyes, those beautiful dark blue eyes that had captivated him from the very first moment he'd met her two years before. "Do you want me to stop?"

He prayed she would say no. And that silent prayer was answered. She slowly shook her head. "It feels—it feels good when you touch me," she admitted.

He groaned, aroused even further by the response. Some women would have done that on purpose, but it was the fact that Georgina didn't know how stimulating her words were that made them even more so.

"I won't do anything that will...ruin you," he promised.

Her eyes flashed with something akin to disappointment, but she didn't answer. She merely cupped the back of his head and drew him down for another of those deep, drugging kisses.

He took that as an agreement and went back to teasing her breast. Her gown was fine, but the silk was very thin and he could feel her nipple tightening, rising to meet him. How he wished he could strip her gown away and see it, memorize its color and shape, its taste. But they had no time for such slow seduction. And the wax exhibit, with all the figures watching them, was not the place.

Resigning himself to that fact, he let his hand drift lower, across her flat stomach and to her hip. She arched a little, murmuring incoherent sounds of encouragement even as her cheeks flushed. Of course they would. No one had ever touched her so intimately. A thought that gave him another shiver of desire.

He ignored it, ignored his own needs, and focused on her. He drew back and watched her as he slid his hand down her leg and began to inch her skirt up. Her eyes went wide, but she did nothing to stop him. Her breath was ragged and her hands trembled.

"You said you wanted something just for you," he whispered. "To do something for your pleasure that would be for no one else."

She nodded, staring at his hand before he slipped it beneath her skirt and started the slow caress back up her calf, her knee. When he touched her thigh, she let out a garbled moan.

"I can give you something just for you. Only you and I will know. I want to do that so much, Georgina. Will you let me?"

She froze as his fingers opened the slit in her drawers and he settled his palm against her sex. He held there, waiting for her permission. Silently pleading for it even though he would withdraw in a heartbeat if she refused.

"Please," she whimpered. "Please do it."

He grinned and moved, letting his index finger trace the slit of her sex gently. She was already wet and so hot against him. He wanted to dive into her, slide his cock to the hilt, claim her.

But there wasn't a place for him there. So all he could do was make her come and store her look, the feel of her sex around him. That would be enough to feed his fantasies for many lonely years to come.

He pressed a thumb against her clitoris and she jolted. She jolted again when he glided one finger into her entrance. She flexed around him, tight and slick, and he nearly came without even being touched.

"God, you are amazing," he murmured, leaning in to kiss her. She relaxed at that now-familiar caress and only when she went limp did he begin to move his finger inside of her. He swirled around her clitoris with his thumb and pumped his finger in time.

Slowly, she began to moan with pleasure at the action. Then she lifted her hips to meet him. He took his time, allowing her to experience the intimacy of this breach, the building pleasure of his touch. He could see her working toward orgasm and he was mesmerized by it.

"Paul," she whispered, her eyes going wide just as she went over the edge. Her body spasmed around his fingers and her back arched as she let out a low, keening cry. He continued to work at her, drawing the pleasure out for both their benefit, and only withdrew when she collapsed, weak and spent, against the settee cushions.

He stared down at her, her eyes filled with satiated drowsiness. She smiled up at him.

"Thank you," she whispered. "Oh, I'm so glad to have felt such a thing."

The words seeped into him. She meant them, of course. He could see that she did. But the reality of what he had just done was becoming increasingly clear. Paul did not act impulsively. He had not done so for years. But touching

Georgina, claiming her, even in this small scale, was impulsive beyond his wildest imaginings.

Now she looked at him in pleasure, but certainly tomorrow she would regret allowing him such liberties. When she took a husband and that man was not the first to pleasure her, she would think of Paul not with kindness, but regret.

What had he been thinking allowing his unrequited feelings for this woman to make him forget his place?

"I'm sorry, Georgina," he murmured as he smoothed her gown back over her legs and stood. He offered her a hand to stand up and she took it with a blank, confused expression.

"Sorry?" she repeated as she watched him back away. He didn't trust himself to stand so close, not when he could smell her on his fingers. Taste her on his lips. "Why are you sorry?"

"I went too far—"

"No!" she gasped out, the high color of release leaving her cheeks in an instant, replaced by chalky paleness.

"Yes, Georgina," he said softly.

She stared at him for a long moment and her emotions flitted across her face as plainly as if they had been written in the darkest ink. He saw pain, disappointment, embarrassment.

He had done this to her. Because he hadn't been in control of himself as he should have been. Because he had wanted to take pleasure from giving her the same. And oh, how he had.

But it had been a selfish act in the end.

"You don't want me." She turned away. "I did something wrong, I'm not experienced enough or pretty enough or—"

He stepped toward her with a gasp. "No, that isn't it." With a shiver, he reached out to touch her arm and turned her to face him once more. "Georgina, I swear to you, there is nothing wrong with you. *I* was wrong."

"But what about everything you said *before*?" she pressed.

He shook his head. "All true, I fear. I do care for you, Georgina. And I did want to do this for you. I wanted to do it for me. But I should have thought it through. I was my duty to you to think it through."

"Paul—" she began, but he cut her off.

"I am a practical man, Georgina. I must be. I know my place in this world and I'm not ashamed of it." He tilted his head, looking at her closely. Drinking her in. "But your father would never accept me."

She sucked in a breath as if she finally understood how deeply Paul cared. He wished she didn't. It made him feel exposed. And it was not a set of emotions that would end in anything but disappointment.

"We could talk to him," she suggested, but her voice was weak.

He smiled at her gently and reached out to trace her silken cheek with his rough finger. "Talk until you are blue, Georgina. We both know he doesn't even like us to be friends, let alone for me to offer for you. And he is right that you deserve more than anything I could give. No, we had this moment." He shook his head. "I *stole* this moment, Georgina. But it was selfish of me to do so and I hope you can forgive me."

She stared at him for so long without speaking that he was about to move on her a second time. But finally she straightened up, steel coming into her eyes, and whispered, "If you want to convince yourself that what just happened was wrong, I certainly am in no position to stop you. But you cannot take away my feelings on this moment we *shared*, not stole. And if you try, Paul Abbot, *that* is what I will never forgive you for."

He was silent, unable to think of what to say to her. But finally she turned away and began to stroll back into the exhibit area.

"Now, I would like to finish my tour, if you don't mind."

He followed her, his heart aching from the passion they had shared and the strength she had exhibited. But mostly from the fact that he loved her, and now that he had let the feeling loose in the world, he realized he could never pretend it didn't exist again.

Georgina smiled at her maid a final time as the girl finished dressing her the next morning.

"Will there be anything else, miss?" Molly asked.

Georgina shook her head. "No. Thank you."

Her maid bobbed out a nod and then slipped from the room, leaving Georgina to stare at herself in the mirror. She hadn't stopped thinking of her night with Paul since it had ended just a few hours ago. No one had been the wiser about her escape and return. At least she didn't believe they had. She could easily just pretend the night had never happened.

Except she wouldn't.

She had played every moment they shared over and over in her head for hours. She hadn't slept, she hadn't stopped and she hadn't been able to keep a burgeoning plan from developing in her mind. A plan she was certain no one in the world would ever approve of.

And yet for the first time, she didn't give a damn. She had finally admitted to herself the truth that had been there all along.

She was in love with Paul Abbot. She had always been attracted to him, of course. But it was more than that. Over the years as they shared more, talked more, as she grew to know him more, attraction had given way to love.

And now that she had experienced his passion, his caring, his regard, she wasn't about to lose it.

She straightened her skirt one last time and marched downstairs to the breakfast room where she knew Annabelle and Marcus awaited her arrival. As she stepped into the room, she stopped. Annabelle was seated at the table and Marcus leaned over her. They were kissing.

For the first time, Georgina understood the passion between them, she understood the love, and she turned away, not in embarrassment, but in jealousy. Her friend already had what Georgina, herself, wanted.

And Georgina was damned well going to try to get the same.

"Oh, goodness," Annabelle said, breaking from Marcus as she noticed Georgina at the door. "I'm sorry, we didn't see you there."

"Clearly," Georgina said, her tone dry as a fall leaf.

Marcus chuckled as he motioned Georgina to a seat. She ignored him and instead paced over to the sideboard as she perused the food she had no interest in eating. This was all an exercise in futility. She was only trying to work up her courage, after all. A tall feat considering she had never allowed herself to have much of that trait.

"Are you well?" Annabelle asked as she stood and took a step toward Georgina. "You look very tired."

Georgina pivoted and looked at her two friends. They cared about her they would not judge her. In truth they were her best and probably only hope. She screwed up her nerve and forced herself to speak at last.

"Do you recall when I foolishly tried to help you with your respectability problem, Annabelle?"

Annabelle blinked and said, "Er, yes. Thank you."

Georgina reached up to press her cold hands against her hot cheeks. "Oh, I'm sorry! I didn't mean it was foolish to help you. More that perhaps the notion of respectability was foolish."

Annabelle moved on her and pulled Georgina's hands away from her face to hold them. "What is going on, Georgina? You seem very upset."

Georgina shook the comforting touch away. She needed to feel her discomfort. It helped drive her on.

"I never understood why you threw everything you could have away on Mr. Rivers." She looked at Marcus, who was shaking his head and laughing at the other end of the table. "Don't misunderstand me, Marcus—you are very handsome, of course. And the more I came to know you, the more I have realized what a truly decent man you are."

He reacted as if physically wounded. "You slander me, woman. I am not decent at all."

Annabelle smiled at his quip. "Oh, hush. Clearly Georgina is upset. Why don't you take your eggs and go bother someone else for a bit."

Georgina shook her head. "Oh no, please don't go! I...I actually need to speak to you both, as humiliating an exercise as this is going to be. You see, I need your help."

Now Marcus straightened up in his chair and the teasing left his eyes. "*Our* help," he repeated. "Georgina what is it? Are you in trouble?"

"No. Yes. Oh, I don't know." She turned away, trying to gather her thoughts. Confession was truly much harder than she'd thought it would be. Especially when her heart and mind were so tangled. "Let me try to explain."

Annabelle motioned her to the table and sat beside her. She laid a hand on hers. "Take your time. We aren't going anywhere."

Marcus nodded as he got up and moved closer to take the place on her other side. The two of them simply stared, waiting.

Georgina took a long, deep breath. "Do you know the wax exhibit has returned to London?"

Annabelle nodded. "Oh yes, I had heard about that. It's wonderful! You should go, you would love it."

Georgina blushed as she pondered what those lifeless wax figures had witnessed just a few hours before. "I wanted to. My father refused to allow it. That was why I was so upset when I came here a few days ago."

"Ah, I had been wondering. You were nearly hysterical when you arrived and then you just left without explanation." Annabelle's brow wrinkled. "I could talk to him. Or arrange for an outing with my brother and Serafina. He would not deny the duke and duchess, would he?"

Georgina shook her head. "I mentioned it to Paul that day, you see," she continued, ignoring Annabelle's suggestion. "And he said he could help me have a private viewing of the collection."

Both Annabelle and Marcus were suddenly silent, staring at Georgina as if she had sprouted a second head which only spoke Latin.

"What? Why do you look at me that way?" she stammered.

Marcus lifted both eyebrows. "Abbot. *Paul Abbot*. Who works for me?"

She nodded. "One and the same."

Annabelle seemed as shocked as her husband apparently was. "I have never known Abbot to break a rule in his life. *Did* he arrange it?"

"Yes." She tried to find her breath but it was becoming almost impossible. "I'm afraid I used my coming here as a ruse. Last night after everyone went to bed, I snuck out to meet him and he took me there."

Marcus's eyes went even wider. "*Paul Abbot.*"

Annabelle shot him a look. "Stop repeating his name, dear. Go on, Georgina."

She clasped her shaking hands before her. "It was wonderful, everything I had hoped it would be. But then Paul admitted…he said… he told me that he has feelings for me."

"Paul Abbot," Marcus muttered, shaking his head in continued disbelief.

"Paul," she reassured him. "Still Paul Abbot."

"And what did you say to him?" Annabelle asked.

"Nothing," she said, softly, as if a whisper would help.

Annabelle's face fell. "Oh, poor Paul. And poor you. How awkward to—"

"No, you misunderstand," Georgina interrupted. "I didn't say nothing because I rejected him. I said nothing because I-I kissed him."

"You *what*?" Marcus and Annabelle exclaimed in unison.

Georgina dropped her gaze to the table and her hands clenched on it. "I-I have also had feelings for him since nearly the first moment we met, you see."

"We are idiots," Annabelle said after a moment of stunned silence had passed between the friends.

"I'm not an idiot," Marcus retorted.

Annabelle glared at him. "Did you know?"

He shrugged. "No."

"Then *we* are idiots," she insisted. "How did we not see? How did Serafina and Gemma and even Mary not see when we are such good friends?"

"What happened next?" Marcus asked.

Georgina blinked, slightly flummoxed by the banter of the couple. Equally turned upside down by what she had to say next. Honesty was her best course of action now, of course, but it was still rather embarrassing to consider it.

"Well, we—he—we—" She struggled, her blush burning her cheeks as she thought of Paul touching her so intimately.

Marcus jumped up from his seat. "Great God! Paul Abbot?"

Georgina turned her face. "Well, we didn't…it didn't go irrevocably far. But things between us *did* turn most passionate."

Annabelle's gentle fingers closed over hers again, and when Georgina dared to look at her, she saw not censure, but understanding and empathy in her friend's bright eyes. Annabelle smiled softly. "How can we help?"

Georgina drew a sharp breath. "I want to be with Paul. I always have—he is my ideal man, you see."

"Paul Abbot?" Marcus said, this time his tone full of questioning that inspired defensiveness in Georgina.

"Yes, Paul Abbot. He and I always have such stimulating conversation. He looks at me and he truly sees me. Other men, they size me up. What could a union with me bring them, what is my dowry, who is my father? Paul just sees me. And he's devilishly handsome, surely even you can see that."

Marcus blinked and Georgina huffed out a breath.

"He *is* handsome," Annabelle reassured her.

"Finally, you two show some reasonability," Georgina sighed. "No one has lived up to Paul's example since the moment I met him. But I always convinced myself he thought nothing of me beyond a bare kindness. Now that I know he cares for me, the situation is increasingly dire."

"Why?" Annabelle encouraged her.

Tears flooded Georgina's eyes. "My father will never allow for anything between Paul and me. He with his Debrett's and his dukes and his earls? He would never accept Paul as my husband, no matter how I pleaded or proved to him that Paul is worthy."

Marcus pinched his lips. "I often do not understand your class," he sniffed.

Annabelle glared at him. "Love, we can discuss the unfairness later. Right now we must focus on Georgina. I don't know how Marcus or I could help convince your father to give you what you wanted. After all, we aren't titled."

"You couldn't," Georgina admitted, ready to get to the most desperate part of her plan. "I would like to arrange for a…a seduction. Paul Abbot and I need to be caught in a compromising position together that will require our marriage. And I need you two to help me arrange it."

Annabelle slipped her hand away with a gasp of shock and Marcus swore as he got up and paced to the window, his back to them.

"Unless you don't approve of the match either?" Georgina asked, suddenly very aware of her failings. "You don't think I'm good enough for Paul?"

"It isn't that," Marcus said, turning on his heel. "When I think of it, your studious, quiet natures would likely suit very well. And if Paul cares for you, if he…somehow allowed something between you to become heated, I would guess that he would like to marry you, too. He would never do such a thing unless he was very serious."

"Then why do you both look so worried?" Georgina asked. She gave Annabelle a pleading look. "Please, tell me."

"A seduction that you are describing could go very wrong," Annabelle said. "And I don't know that Paul would go along with it. He is so very honorable. A wonderful quality, of course, but I don't see him forcing something like this even for the best cause."

Georgina folded her arms. "I realize that. Which is why he wouldn't know what I was doing. Then he will be blameless."

"And likely furious," Marcus said, shaking his head.

"I would rather have him furious and mine than have to marry some stuffy marquis while I pine for him forever," Georgina snapped as she jumped up. "I have been doing what everyone else wants, what everyone else requires for years. I don't want to live the rest of my life regretting it. I will make it up to him afterward, but please, please won't you help me?"

Marcus looked past her, his eyes locking with Annabelle's. Unspoken communication flowed between them as Georgina held her breath and hoped they would come out on her side after all.

Finally, Marcus sighed. "I do owe him. After all, he helped orchestrate something quite similar for Annabelle."

Georgina's eyes went wide and she jerked her gaze to her friend, who was merely smiling. "Indeed, he did."

"Very well, Georgina," Marcus said. "We will help you. And I know exactly the best place to shock your father into action."

CHAPTER SIX

Paul couldn't keep the scowl from his face as he strode through the empty main hall of the Donville Masquerade. In a few hours, the place would be buzzing with patrons gambling and also relieving their sexual tensions right in the open for everyone to see.

Normally Paul barely even noticed such things. They had become commonplace in his world and he kept his own desires far separate from the ones expressed here. But since his powerful encounter with Georgina a few days earlier, he had become more and more irritated by the passions exhibited in this hall.

Why should all these people get what they wanted while his desires remained forever out of reach?

"Mr. Abbot," said Cord, the butler for the hell, as he puffed and struggled to keep up with Paul's long stride.

He came to a sudden stop and Cord nearly toppled over with the unexpected ceasing of motion.

"What is it?" Paul asked, hating how sharp his tone was. Marcus was the roaring bear here, Paul had always been the one to maintain calm.

Now fulfilling that role felt almost impossible.

"Sir, we have been waiting for your arrival. Mr. Rivers has requested some changes in the purple salon and they require your attention."

Paul pursed his lips as he withdrew the small notebook he always carried from his breast pocket. "Cord, today I must do the following list of things."

He turned the paper so the butler could see the three pages of notes he had taken the night before. He'd been hoping work would help him forget Georgina. It hadn't thus far, but he had little other recourse.

"It is a long list, I see," Cord said.

"Is it possible someone else could see to Marcus's whims just this once?" he asked, grinding his teeth.

Cord's eyes went wide at the uncharacteristic temper Paul was displaying. But then he shook his head, singular in his direction. "I'm afraid not, sir. Mr. Rivers told me you would need to see to it yourself. I am just the messenger, Mr. Abbot."

Paul froze at that last admonishment, spoken softly by the ever-loyal servant. He took a long breath and exhaled before he spoke again.

"You are correct, Cord. I'm sorry for my bad humor. I have a great deal on my mind, most of it having nothing to do with the Masquerade. I shouldn't take it out on you regardless of the source of my discontent. I'll see to Rivers' changes and, in the meantime, will you be certain the deliveries were made this morning? We've been having trouble getting the spirits stocked before we open and it vexes me."

Cord let out a brisk nod. "Certainly, sir. I'll see to it right away."

The butler scuttled off to do as asked, and Paul sighed. He had never felt such frustration in his life. Swiftly he turned down a long hallway that led to the hell's private rooms. Once the club was open, these were rooms where ladies and gentleman of all rank and richness could act out their deepest fantasies.

He was not surprised to find the door to the purple salon open and waiting for him. He entered and looked toward the table beside the bed for a list of changes to be made, but the sound of the door closing behind him made him turn.

Leaning against the door was Georgina.

He blinked a few times, hoping to clear this addlepated dream from his line of vision. He wanted her so much he had conjured a hallucination of her here—that was the only explanation. God, how he hoped it was.

Except that she didn't disappear as he had anticipated would happen. She just stood there, watching him, her hands shaking at her sides.

"Damn Marcus," he muttered. "I should have known he would repay me for Annabelle at some point."

Her eyes went wide. "Are you referring to their courtship here?"

He frowned. "Told you about it, did they? Well, I'd hardly call it a courtship, though it did lead them to be wed." He blinked, and still she remained. "What are you doing here, Georgina—Miss Hickson?"

She flinched at his correction to the formality between them. Formality he never should have allowed to fall since he obviously had no control over himself when it came to this woman. Even now, looking at her from across a room, all he could see was how beautiful she was in a dark blue gown that matched her eyes.

God how he wanted to kiss her again. To touch her again. To claim her this time as he hadn't at the wax exhibit. He shook his head.

"I came here because I wanted to see you," she said, her voice shaking but without hesitation. "Paul, all I have thought about since that night at Madame Tussaud's is you."

He squeezed his eyes shut at her confession. How tempting she was, without even trying to be. But he had to resist for both their sakes. "This is not a proper place for you."

"If you are here, it is the most proper place for me," she insisted. "Look at me, Paul."

He slowly opened his eyes and did as she asked. It was a torture.

"Paul, I am in love with you," she whispered. "I have been

forever. I cannot pretend it away anymore."

Her words crashed into him like a wave on a rocky shore and he nearly toppled over in shock and joy that she had said them. Georgina loved him, just as he loved her. But reality followed on the heels of fantasy and everything that would keep them apart ripped his happiness to pieces.

"You *must* pretend," he insisted as he moved on her. "For we cannot be together, and you know why. Now let me take you out of here before you—"

He cut himself off as his hand closed around her upper arm. She gazed up at him, blue eyes hazy with desire and love. Touching her had been a wicked mistake and now he was snared by her siren's call.

"Georgina," he whispered, both a plea and a warning. Why wouldn't she step away when he couldn't?

"Paul," she whispered in return, and reached up to stroke the back of her bare hand across his cheek.

He couldn't maintain a handle on control any longer. He dipped his head and kissed her, wrapping his arms around her, drawing her to him, molding her against him as tightly as he could without stripping her bare and joining their bodies. It wasn't enough. And it was too much.

She lifted into his kiss and returned it with fervor and fever. Her heated tongue lapping at his closed lips stripped away the last vestiges of gentlemanly behavior and he made a strangled curse as he backed her toward the bed in the middle of the room. They fell across it and he cupped her breast as she arched beneath him, their mouths still desperately mating.

"Georgina," he managed to rasp as he broke the kiss. "Please. I can't stop this, so *you* must. For your own good."

She stared up at him, and he held his breath as he waited for her to ask him to get off her. She had to come to her senses, after all. It was their only hope.

But instead, without breaking her gaze, she reached up and unfastened the buttons along the front of her gown. She parted the fabric and revealed a very pretty but rather sheer chemise beneath.

"No," he whispered, but could not make himself move. She reached out and took his hand, and guided it to her nearly naked flesh.

"Yes," she insisted. "Please. Now."

He growled out desire so powerful that he could have torn her apart with it and ground his mouth back to hers as he squeezed the breast offered to him like a feast to a starving man.

She gasped into his mouth and arched into him as he began to pluck one hard nipple with his thumb, over and over, in a rhythm that he had designed to drive her wild. Her hips began to rise and fall in time to his touch, her breath short and hot against his lips.

He wanted to lick her, he wanted to stroke her, he wanted to press himself inside of her and make her moan his name. There had never been another woman to make him feel so animal in his desire. And there had never been another woman to make him feel so tender in his love for her.

He knew it wasn't possible, but his heart and his body led him in a different direction from his screaming mind. And they were far more powerful in this moment.

He dragged his mouth away from hers, down her throat, down across her collarbone, until he latched on to the same nipple he had been teasing with his thumb.

"Oh my God," she grunted as he sucked her hard through the sheer fabric, swirled his tongue around her, gave her exactly what he knew she needed without even asking. Because he knew her and he loved her and there was a bond between them that gave him answers without having to ask questions.

"Paul," she groaned, her hands threading through his hair, holding him against her as she shivered with building pleasure.

He began to ratchet her skirts up, his hand trembling as he did it. He'd been dreaming of her slick, tight heat since the last time he touched her intimately, and now he couldn't resist it.

"Let me touch you," she breathed, her fingers trailing

down to drag alone the front of his trouser flap.

The feel of her hands, even through the heavy fabric, was almost too much to take. He thrust his hips toward her with a low moan and she smiled up at him in a combination of understanding and triumph.

God, how he loved her.

He shoved that thought aside along with the thoughts that followed about how desperate that feeling was and instead delved into kissing her as his fingers finally found the slick entrance of her sex.

"God," he murmured against her mouth. "You are a revelation."

"Please, won't you take me?" she asked, gasping as he stroked over her the same way he had in the wax museum. "Make me yours in a way no one can take away, no one can change."

He pulled back and stared down at her. Her eyes were glossy with unshed tears and want, her breath short from desire. She was a wicked, heartbreaking temptation.

"Georgina," he whispered, trying to get up the ability to pull away as he knew he should.

But before he could do that, the door behind them flew open. Paul pivoted, rolling to block the intruder's view of Georgina's half-naked body in the bed.

His jaw dropped open, his eyes widened, for there in the entryway, his face turning purple, was Georgina's father, flanked on one side by Marcus.

"Just what the hell do you think you're doing?" Hickson roared.

CHAPTER SEVEN

Georgina had been perfectly aware that being caught in this position by her father would be embarrassing. But as she tugged her bodice up and smoothed her skirts down to cover herself, she was almost swept away by the humiliation. Her father just stood there, angry, puffing like a bull and staring at her as if she had stolen something.

"What the hell are you thinking, Georgina? Coming to this…this disgusting place without a maid and letting this fortune hunter trick you into a bed?" he barked as he strode fully into the room.

Marcus quietly followed and shut the door behind them. He silently leaned back against the barrier, unspeaking but in a stance of wary readiness. Georgina flashed him a quick, grateful look before she drew a breath and answered her father.

"Father—"

But he clearly didn't give a damn about her answer, for he continued to rail. "Your mother and I have done everything to protect you during your Seasons. We've done everything to shield you from those who would take advantage. And this is the thanks we get? You ungrateful child!"

Now that she was covered, Paul got to his feet and held up a hand. "Mr. Hickson, you mustn't blame your daughter," he began.

Georgina jumped up. "You must very much blame your

daughter," she corrected. "I am not a child who didn't understand what I was doing, Paul. Don't disregard this as a foolish, youthful mistake. I know my mind and I know my heart."

Paul sent her a quick look. "Georgina, please. Don't make this worse than it is."

Her father moved on him. "You shut your mouth. I don't blame my daughter, sir, I blame *you*. For two years I have watched you with her. I have seen your sideways glances and the longing in your stare. And I knew it wasn't her charms or her beauty which tempted you. Admit it, you have always been drawn in by her money and her ties to a family of such importance."

Paul's face twisted in horror at the accusation and Georgina flew between the men, offering herself as a shield between her father's ugly words and Paul's very decent true self.

"Stop, Father!" she burst out. "Stop this at once. You don't understand. I am in love with this man. I am in love with Paul Abbot."

She had somehow hoped that this declaration would shock her father into seeing the truth. But instead of softening, he shook his head.

"Of course he would make you believe that—he would play on your weak, romantic heart." There was no malice to his tone, despite his harsh words. There was only sadness. "He is using you, daughter, and the fact that I have caught you here only proves it. He is trying to force you into a union that will benefit only himself."

Marcus finally cleared his throat, and all heads in the room swiveled to him. He kept his gaze firmly on Georgina as he said, "Actually, Mr. Hickson, you are correct. This entire exchange *was* orchestrated. You were meant to find Georgina here with my manager. But Abbot had nothing to do with it. Georgina was the master of this plot."

Georgina caught her breath. She hadn't expected Marcus

to reveal her machinations like that, but as she met his gaze she saw why. She *had* to admit what she had done both to clear Paul's name and to let both her father and her lover know how deeply serious she was about forging a future that followed her heart, rather than the rules her parents had endlessly forced upon her.

Her father and Paul both turned back to her, and she almost laughed. Their expressions were twin images of horror and betrayal. As if this experience and their shock and eventual anger with her would bond them.

Paul was the first one to find his voice, it seemed. "Why would you do something so drastic and foolish, Georgina?"

She shook her head. "You know why, Paul. I am in love with you. Deeply and truly in love with you." His hard expression softened a fraction, but it seemed to be against his will. She turned away from it and toward her father. "I have lived under your rules for years, Father. I knew you would never let me have this man without drastic intervention. And this was the best plan I could concoct on short notice and under duress."

Her father's eyes were wide and his hands shook. When he spoke, his voice was low and strained. "You would go so far to escape my protection?"

She swallowed, captivated by the true pain on his face. He had spent so much time in the past few years growing increasingly frustrated and disappointed in her and her failure to do as he expected. But this look on his face, this was something different. There was…there was *love* there. And she didn't think she'd seen that for a very long time.

She nodded as she fought to find her voice again. "I am so sorry to cause you pain or humiliation, Father…*Papa*. But you…you do not listen to me when I speak to you about what I want. You don't *hear* me. So I knew I couldn't just tell you the truth, I had to shock you with it."

Her father turned his face, his cheeks pale and his gaze filled with chagrin. "I-I only want what is best for you,

Georgina."

"But you cannot think that I could decide what is best for myself," she whispered.

He walked a few steps away. When he turned back, his mouth was pinched in a thin line. "You don't understand. When you first came out, do you know how many offers I had for you?"

She blinked. "I have never had an offer, Father. We both know that. It is why you have come to despise me so deeply."

He shook his head. "No, no, not at all. I should have told you the truth. Let me try now." He scrubbed a hand over his face. "You have a large dowry, as you know." He shot Paul a glare. "As *everyone* knows. And while it was put in place to help you, your mother and I quickly came to realize it also put you in danger. Within a few weeks of your first debut, we had offers from several men, and we were pleased. But upon deeper inspection, we came to realize that they were all after your money. They didn't give a damn about you. There were titled scoundrels who had lost it all, social climbers who pretended to be something they weren't. It was a rogues gallery, and we were disgusted at the idea of turning our dearest daughter over to a man like that."

She drew back. "I—why didn't you tell me?"

He snorted out a humorless laugh. "You were always so quiet, so uncertain of yourself and what you had to offer. What good would telling you those awful things have done? I feared you would retreat into your shell further."

"So you pushed me to present a more perfect picture in order to..." She trailed off as recognition dawned on her.

He nodded. "To obtain a man who truly deserved you, my dear. But now...I want the best for you, Georgina. And I can't stand by and watch you marry a fortune hunter who has convinced you that his feelings for you are tender."

Paul took a gulp of air, his eyes narrowing, but before he could launch into a tirade at her father, Marcus stepped forward instead.

"Mr. Hickson, I don't know if my opinion is of any value to you, but Abbot is the most faithful and honest man I have ever had the pleasure to know. I would never for a moment believe him to be a fortune hunter."

"Says his employer, a man who runs this utterly vulgar club," Georgina's father snapped, and Georgina shot Marcus an apologetic look.

It seemed unnecessary, for he only shrugged. "Then why don't you ask some of the men Paul Abbot served with in India?"

Her father's forehead wrinkled. "India?"

Marcus nodded. "This 'fortune hunter', as you call him, served with distinction in the East India Company and was injured saving ten other men in his company, including the son of the Earl of Waterberg. I will tell you all of those men will say nothing but good about him. I know that for a fact because I spoke to them ten years ago before I took Abbot into my employ."

Paul had been curiously silent during the exchange, but now he moved toward Marcus, his eyes wide and his face lined with the same remnants of pain she had seen on them when he told her a portion of his history in the wax exhibit.

"You—you knew?" he stammered.

Marcus smiled, and it was a warm expression that spoke volumes of how deeply he cared for Paul. "I know everything. Always."

Paul was silent for a long moment. Then he slowly turned his attention back to Georgina. In his eyes, she saw a shift. A determination that fanned the hope in her heart like nothing before. It was as if he had finally made a decision and there was nothing that would stop him now.

"Georgina," he said softly, saying her name as an endearment like there was no one in the room but them. "Do you truly love me?"

She nodded without hesitation. "Yes. I am absolutely, without a doubt, in love with you, Paul Abbot." Then she bit her lip. "But—but you have never said the same. You told me you cared for me, not loved me."

She waited for him to say something, to admit his heart in return, but instead, he turned away from her to her father.

"Sir, I am not a fortune hunter. I may not have anything close to your annual income, but I have invested well and can keep your daughter more than comfortable. I would *never* ask for her dowry. In fact, I would insist you keep it. Or at least put it into an account that only she controls. My intentions are the best they can be."

Georgina watched her father, but his face was impassive and she couldn't read his reaction to Paul's suggestion. His voice was very hard as he said, "Your intentions? How can you speak of me of your intentions when you have her in this club like a whore?"

Georgina flinched. "Don't forget, Father, I came here. He didn't ask me."

Paul shot her a glance. "What your daughter says is true, and yet I understand your question of my intentions. After all, I may not have brought her here, but I most definitely went too far. Once I found her here, I should have had the strength to turn her away when she threw herself into my arms. But I didn't. I-I am in love with Georgina, sir. And that made getting swept away far too easy." He sighed. "But I did not claim her—I didn't ruin her. So if you decide that I am not worthy of her hand, despite my feelings for her and hers for me, you needn't worry that this story will leave this hall. I wouldn't interfere in her future or ever do anything to bring her grief."

She blinked at the tears that filled her eyes. "Except offer to walk away from me when I love you more than anything?"

"If that would give you the best chance at happiness, I would." His voice cracked on the last two words and she could see his pain. It mirrored hers. And yet here they waited for her father's approval. Because Paul Abbot was a decent man and he would not take what was not given freely.

Even if she tried to force her father's hand, Paul would

not.

She turned to her father with a long sigh. "Then I suppose you hold my fate, as always. What do you say, Father?"

He was quiet for a very long time. So long that she nearly broke into tears. He stared at Paul, he stared at her, and finally he asked, "You would marry this man if there were no impediments?"

She nodded immediately. "If Paul asked me, I would say yes with no hesitation and only joy in my heart."

Her father's eyes fluttered shut. "Oh, Georgina."

She moved forward and took one of his clenched fists in her hand. The action forced her father to look at her and she prayed he could see her sincerity and Paul's as she whispered, "I love you, Papa. And I have truly tried to make you happy, but there has been no man to tempt me in the four Seasons I have trod the London halls. And since I met this man..."

She released her father and stepped back to now take Paul's hand. He allowed it and squeezed gently as she looked up into his impossibly handsome, wonderful face.

"Since I met this man I knew there would be no other for me," she finished.

"And you, Abbot, would you marry her?"

Now Georgina held her breath once more. Paul could deny her in some twisted attempt to protect her, to provide her with a future she no longer desired. A future she knew now she would never take, even if it were offered to her on a silver platter by a duke of the highest order.

Paul smiled, his expression very soft. "Yes. With your permission, sir, I would make her my wife. With great pleasure and with no other motive than to make her happy for all the rest of our days."

Her knees went weak at that agreement, not made reluctantly but with joy and hope on his stern face. She longed to kiss him, but didn't. Not with her father already so very angry.

She forced herself to look to her father again, and he

nodded. With a great sigh, he said, "Then you have my blessing, for I have only ever wanted my daughter to be happy. And I can see the only path to her happiness is the same path which leads to you."

Georgina could no more control the cry of joy that burst from her lips than she could control the act of breathing. She flew at her father. "Truly?"

He nodded, and for a moment she saw hope for her reflected in his eyes. "Yes," he repeated. Then he glared at Paul and motioned to the bed. "But no more of this until you are lawfully wed."

Paul moved forward and took her hand. With the other, he offered a handshake to her father. "Of course, sir. I would not think of betraying your trust again."

Her father hesitated, but then reached out and shook Paul's hand. "Now Mr. Rivers and I will leave you two to finish fixing yourselves." He glared at Paul again. "*Quickly*, you understand."

Paul nodded. "Certainly, sir. We won't be but a moment."

Her father hesitated, but then turned and motioned Marcus to the door. "Come, sir. I have heard this club stocks some of the best whisky in the city. I think I have earned a glass, both to recover from my shock and to celebrate my daughter's upcoming union."

"I will buy you one myself," Marcus said with a laugh, opening the door and gesturing Georgina's father out before he gave a big wink to Georgina and Paul and shut them in alone again.

The moment they were gone, Paul turned on her. He grasped the front of her dress, which still half gaped after their near-love making. He tugged it shut and began to button her as he glared down at her.

"Georgina Hickson, you lied to me," he murmured. "And I think we need to discuss it."

Paul stared down into Georgina's beautiful, blue upturned eyes. They were filled with joy. The same joy he felt at the idea that this woman would soon be his wife. But her methods...those he did not approve of.

"What do you have to say for yourself?" he asked, trying to keep his tone firm when what he wanted to do was sweep her against him and kiss her silly as a celebration of their very happy news.

She dropped her lashes demurely. "I am sorry, Paul. I realize I put you in a terrible position."

He stifled a groan as he thought of the "position" they had been in before they were interrupted. And very soon they would be there again, only this time with nothing stopping him from claiming her.

But of course she meant his position with her father.

"What I don't understand is why you didn't simply write to me, explain yourself. We could have designed a plan together."

She hesitated. "I suppose I simply feared you would refuse me. Not because you didn't care for me or want me—I knew you were too good a man to go so far with me if you didn't feel something beyond mere lust. But because you are so proud and so decent that you wouldn't agree to such subterfuge."

"You are right, I would not have, and do not believe in such trickery." He frowned. "Georgina, you could have done permanent damage to yourself, and if your father hadn't bowed to your convincing, you could have destroyed any chance of us being together."

She arched a brow. "Does that mean you would have approached him yourself, if I hadn't pushed the issue?"

He hesitated. It was a good question. He'd been thinking of nothing but Georgina since the night they shared at Madame Tussaud's, but he hadn't the courage to think they could be happy together.

Not like she had.

"You must think me a coward," he said.

She cupped his cheek, her skin impossibly soft on his. "Never."

"Since my return from India I have been...cautious. Perhaps too cautious. But I tell you now, Georgina, I knew I loved you, and I think that eventually I would have tried to convince your father of my heart and my intentions. In my own time."

She slid her hand from his cheek and wrapped both arms around his neck. "Are you very, very angry with me for rushing your schedule? For taking this situation into my own hands?"

He couldn't continue to be severe with her. Not when she looked up at him with such joy and devotion. Not when she was suddenly and inexplicably his thanks to her wild scheming.

"I am not angry," he admitted. "Because you have given me exactly what I have wanted since the very first moment you walked into the room at Annabelle and Marcus's party two years ago."

"Did you truly love me then?" she whispered.

He nodded. "Truly. I wanted to dismiss it, but the more I got to know you, the greater friends we somehow became, the more that feeling has grown, no matter how I tried to diminish it. I love you, Georgina. And I cannot tell you how happy I am in this moment."

She smiled, her face lighting up as it hadn't in the entire time he had known her. He realized that the weight of her time in Society had been lifted from her slender shoulders. And now she was left with only happiness and joy and a certainty in their future.

"But there is one more thing I must do before we join your father and Marcus," he said.

She shook her head. "What is that?"

He dropped down on one knee and stared up at her.

"Georgina Hickson, will you do me the great honor and equally intense pleasure of being my wife?"

"I have already agreed—" she began.

He shook his head. "No, we both told your father that if we were free to marry, we would. But I did not formally ask you if you would take my hand, if you would join my life, if you would accept what little I have to offer not just today, but for all the days we have left. Georgina, will you marry me?"

Tears had leapt into her eyes, but they were obviously tears of happiness. She smiled through them with all her love for him shining clear on her face.

"Yes, Paul Abbot. I will marry you. And I will endeavor not to drive you utterly mad for the rest of your life."

He pushed back to his feet and drew her into his arms. "My love, I fully expect and look forward to being driven mad. Every day. Every blessed, perfect day."

Then he dropped his mouth to hers and kissed her.

EPILOGUE

Two months later

Georgina ran her brush through her hair as she looked at herself in the mirror. She was, finally and forever, Mrs. Paul Abbot. If she had thought herself happy on the day he had proposed to her in the club, now she was ecstatic. So much had changed since that desperate afternoon.

The door to her new chamber opened, and in the mirror, she watched Paul step through, his gaze falling on her and his smile widening.

"My parents have departed?" she asked as she got to her feet and turned to face him.

She was wearing a very pretty, very sheer night shift under her robe, but she was feeling a little nervous to reveal it. After all, Paul had been nothing but gentlemanly since their engagement, so they had not touched in an intimate way, save a few stolen kisses, in two months. Though she did often catch him looking at her with a certain hungry look.

A hunger she echoed at night in her empty bed.

"At last, yes," he said with a happy sigh. "With all their good wishes."

She smiled. "You have proven yourself to them, Paul. All your attention to their concerns, the way you have addressed them all so carefully over the weeks, it made such a difference. This morning as we were riding over to the church, both of them waxed poetic about you. If you ever worried about garnering their approval, you have done that and even more."

He nodded. "Yes, it seems so, though I know they both still hesitate about the club—not that I can blame them. Either way, I am pleased, for I never wanted them to look on me as the fortune hunter your father once accused me of being."

She shook her head. "They don't anymore. And I never have, and as your wife, I would say mine is the only opinion that will ever matter."

"Been talking to Annabelle, have we?" he teased as he moved toward her slowly.

She laughed, though her nervousness was beginning to increase as he reached out to stroke his fingers across the exposed skin of her wrist.

"I do like it when you say the word *wife*," he said, his voice getting rougher. "Won't you say it again?"

She leaned in and whispered, "*Wife*."

"Yes," he groaned. "Wife. My wife. And now I would very much like to consummate this union at last."

She blushed. Paul was usually very proper, but now there was a dark and dangerous look to him. One that made her thighs clench as she remembered the intense pleasure he had given her not so very long ago.

"I've been waiting for this," she whispered as she finally dared to loosen her dressing gown. With hands shaking, she slid it away and tossed it aside to stand before him in the short, sheer gown beneath.

"Good God," he groaned, not moving but just staring at her for a very long moment. "You are beautiful."

She smiled. Paul always made her *feel* beautiful. And now he was going to love her with his body as he had been for weeks with his words and his precious gestures.

"Will you...will you..."

She trailed off, unable to ask the question that was on her lips. He stepped toward her and glided just one finger beneath the thin strap of her chemise.

"Will I?" he encouraged her.

She took a long breath. "Will you remove your clothing this time? The last two times you weren't able, and I admit I've been very curious. Mother wasn't helpful in that arena, although Serafina and Annabelle and Gemma have given me some good advice in the past few weeks."

He laughed. "I'm certain that is true. And yes, Georgina, I will remove my clothing tonight. I want to feel my body pressed against yours. I want to touch you in every way and I want to allow you to touch me. In fact—"

He cut himself off and stepped back to remove his jacket, then loosened his cravat. Slowly, he unfastened the crisp white shirt beneath and slid it away until he stood before her in only his trousers.

She caught her breath. Paul had always had a certain wiry strength to him. She had felt the muscles beneath his clothes when they danced or she stole a moment to kiss him. But now...now she could see him half-naked, and he was better than she'd ever imagined.

He was a finely defined man, with lean muscle at his stomach, strong arms and perfectly formed shoulders. Well, one perfectly formed shoulder. The other was scarred terribly.

She stepped forward and hesitantly allowed her hand up to touch the flesh mangled long ago. He allowed it, watching her closely.

"Does it still hurt?" she whispered.

He nodded slowly. "Not the flesh, but the damage beneath occasionally aches. Not so that I cannot do what I wish, but there is discomfort."

She met his eyes. "I am sorry for that. And so proud of your bravery in saving others."

Now it was his turn to blush and dart his gaze away. "I am half-naked now, Georgina. It is time to remove that very pretty night shift."

She smiled and stepped closer, letting her body just brush his. "Then *I* will be completely naked. It seems unfair."

He put his hand beneath her gown straps and glided them down at the same time. "It seems perfect," he retorted as the gown pooled at her feet and she stood before him in nothing more than her skin.

She had never been naked with him. She'd always had some tiny protection of her gown, as bunched and lifted as it had been. But she found she wasn't awkward as he stared, his eyes lit up with fire. No, she felt nothing but powerful, beautiful, *his*.

"I have waited for this," he growled as his hands slid down her arms, cupped her hips. "I have imagined it for years."

"Well, I'm here. And I'm yours," she reminded him. "For always."

He nodded, but surprised her by stepping back. Swiftly he toed off his boots, and removed his trousers in lightning speed. Her eyes widened as he straightened up and she saw a man naked, *her* man naked, for the first time.

His...member—a cock, Annabelle had called it when she tried to explain what would happen on Georgina's wedding night—was very large. And it was already hard.

"It will fit?" she asked, needing a little reassurance even though the sight of him like this was exciting.

"It will. And by the time it does, you will be ready for it." He reached for her hand and guided her to their bed. The firelight danced off the coverlet and she shivered as he urged her to lie across it.

He took a place beside her, lying on his side to face her.

"You liked what happened before?" he asked.

She nodded. "Yes. Sometimes I would try to touch myself as you had touched me in the wax exhibit and found some echo of the pleasure, but never quite the same," she admitted.

His eyes fluttered shut. "You don't know what you do to me," he muttered, almost more to himself than to her. When he looked at her again, he was smiling. "I'll repeat that and more, Georgina. I promise you."

He leaned over her and lowered his mouth to hers. She

lifted into him, wrapped her arms around his neck, relaxing into the pleasure of his deep, probing kiss. When she sighed and shivered against him, he broke the kiss and glided lower, letting his mouth move against her throat, her collarbone. Finally, he settled his lips against her breast, just as she had been dreaming about him doing since the day of their engagement.

His tongue swirled around her, blurring her vision and making her back arch as she moaned with pleasure. It was amazing that when he touched her elsewhere on her body, her sex responded so strongly. She tingled between her legs and she felt hot moisture beginning to pool there.

He shifted to the opposite breast, sucking hard enough that she gasped and her fingers tangled in his hair to encourage more of the sharp, focused pleasure.

He looked up at her, his dark eyes focused on her face even as he continued to lick and suck her. She locked gazes with him, the intensity between them making the sensations even more powerful.

He smiled against her flesh and then he moved again, his mouth moving over her stomach. Her eyes went wide. He wasn't going to...he couldn't...

He gently parted her legs with his warm hands and settled between them. He said nothing, but stared at her sex as if memorizing the look of her. She tensed as he traced her entrance with just the tip of his finger. Then he shocked her by burying his mouth against her and kissing her in that most intimate place.

At first the kisses were chaste and closed-mouthed. But soon he darted his tongue out to trace her slit. And his fingers joined in the torture, spreading her lips open, giving him better access.

If she had felt heat and wetness gathering there before, now there was nothing but lightning bolts of intense sensation. She lifted her hips toward him and he chuckled as he swirled his tongue around the tiny little bundle of nerves at the top of her sex. What had Annabelle called that? Her clitoris?

Well, he had found it, and now he was suckling it as he had done with her nipple. Only the sensation he created was far more powerful, far more intense. She found herself flexing her sex in time, her breath coming short, her vision blurring, and suddenly she was on the edge of ultimate pleasure.

"Please," she panted, staring at him, grinding against him to find release. "Please."

He sucked even harder, and she couldn't stop the keening cry that escaped her lips as little explosions of pleasure rocked her, spiraling forever, making her body shake out of her control. And he gave her no quarter as she shook beneath him, continuing the assault of his mouth until she flopped, spent against the pillows.

He rose back up her body, braced himself over her and stared down into her face. "You are so sweet," he drawled.

She shivered as she realized he was talking about her flavor, an intimate knowledge only he would ever have. The thought thrilled her.

"And now will you, will we...will you claim me?" she asked, still panting from release.

He smiled, his expression soft. "Yes. At last."

He settled between her still-spread legs, positioning himself carefully. She felt the nudge of his cock at her slick entrance and waited for the breech. But instead, he simply stared down at her.

"I love you, Georgina," he whispered. "There may be a little pain, but I promise you I will go slowly."

"You couldn't hurt me," she said softly as she cupped the back of his neck and drew him down for a kiss. "Right now I could fly."

Their lips met, and she tasted her own earthly flavor on his tongue. She was so enraptured by it, so aroused by it, that she hardly noticed him move. Then he was sliding inside of her, slowly, gently. Her eyes went wide as there was a burst of pain, and he stilled immediately.

"And now I'm yours," she said, trying to relax against him. It was truly more odd than painful now. She felt very full with his big hardness inside her. Full, and yet it was also an anxious feeling. Like she was waiting for something.

For him to move.

"Are you ready?" he asked. "Because you won't be mine until you quake around me."

She shivered. So he could give her pleasure this way, too? It seemed the possibilities were endless, and she couldn't help but thrill at the thought of exploring each and every one now that they were free to do so.

"I'm ready," she assured him.

He slid forward again, further and further, until he was fully seated in her body. He stopped once more, his voice strained as he groaned, "My God, you are tight. So perfect."

She shifted beneath him and an electric shot of pleasure arced through her. Her eyes went wide as she looked up at him. She flexed her hips again, and he made an almost pained sound.

"I'm trying to be gentle," he said, his voice heavy with strain. "But you're making it very difficult."

"Then don't try," she whispered. "Please, please..."

He didn't force her to finish the question she wasn't certain how to ask. He just began to move inside her. He was slow at first, grinding his hips in small circles as he took her. And the pleasure she had felt from his lips flashed back to life. She clenched his shoulders, gasping for air as his thrusts began to be a little harder, a little faster.

Pleasure was like an approaching wave. She felt it coming, she wanted it to crash over her, and yet when it did, she yelped in surprise as much as relief, clinging to him as he continued to take her in those long, strong strokes.

His face twisted in pleasure, his lips pressing together, his neck strained, and finally, with a cry of her name that echoed in the room, he stroked one final time and she felt his hot seed move within her.

He collapsed over her and she clung to him, reveling in his weight, in his heat and in the fact that at last she was truly and fully his.

Finally, he moaned and moved off her, gathering her to his side and into his arms.

"Was that all right?" he asked when both of them had caught their breath. "Was I too rough?"

She laughed against his chest at the idea that her moans and cries of pure pleasure could be misconstrued as anything else. "It is funny you ask me that, because I was just thinking that *this* was what the fuss was about. If I had known, I might have snuck out my window weeks ago and come to you, rules be damned."

He chuckled as he pressed a kiss to her forehead. "I would not have denied you, I cannot say otherwise. But now we are wed and I can have you however and whenever and wherever I would like."

She rolled over and perched herself on his chest where she could look into his eyes. "That sounds very promising. You mean there is more to learn?"

He swallowed hard. "Oh, so much more, Georgina. And I'm going to teach you, and I'm going to learn what you like and what makes you quake and what makes you scream."

"I very much look forward to it, Mr. Abbot."

"I very much look forward to every part of our life together, Mrs. Abbot," he answered as he leaned forward. "Because I am so utterly in love with you."

Then he kissed her and she lost all her retorts, all her agreements, everything but how deeply she loved him. And how happy she knew she would be for the rest of her days.

A Marquis for Mary
(THE NOTORIOUS FLYNNS BOOK 5)

By

Jess Michaels

CHAPTER ONE

1816

Once upon a time, Mary Quinn had loved a ball. She had chosen her gowns with a thrill in her heart. She'd swept in and smiled as her name was announced. She had bounced on the tips of her toes as she watched the bustle around her, eager to take part in the romance she thought existed in the wide, wonderful world.

But it had been nearly four years since her first ball, four long and unfruitful Seasons looking for a husband, and the shine had entirely worn off the endeavor. Now she stood to the side of the dance floor, trying desperately not to let her mouth turn down in a deep frown.

It wasn't that what she was seeing around her was so very awful. In fact, her observations made her incredibly happy. Her eyes first fell on her beloved older sister Gemma, who had married two years before. Gemma's eyes were lit up as she looked up into the equally loving gaze of her husband Crispin.

As they twirled away, a new couple came into view, Crispin's brother Rafe and his wife Serafina, the model of a devoted couple if there ever was one.

Once more the crowd shifted and now Crispin and Rafe's sister Annabelle and her husband Marcus came into view. Marcus looked at his wife like he could kiss her right then and there, despite the shock such a thing would cause.

One final time, the crowd moved and Mary's good friend Georgina spun by in the arms of her recent fiancé, Paul Abbot, who worked for Marcus.

Each of the couples, all her family and friends, were completely happy and utterly in love. Mary had once wanted the same. Two years ago, when she had been taken from the very unhappy home of her father and into Crispin and Gemma's house, she had dared to again believe that love might happen for her, too. But now they were in the middle of her fourth Season and…still there was no love on the horizon. No suitor at all, loving or not, had made himself clear.

Which under normal circumstances would be embarrassing, but in her case, struck terror in her heart. Her father had begun to make noises about Mary returning to his home, to his control. He wanted her married and he had proven not once but twice with Gemma that he would sell his daughters to the highest bidder. It was doubtful Mary would be happy in his choices.

"I am running out of time," she whispered to herself as she willed tears of fear and frustration not to fall. People would talk if she began weeping in the middle of the gathering, and that was the last thing she needed.

She turned away from the dance floor in an effort to control her suddenly bubbling emotions and moved across the ballroom toward a table that held refreshments. But before she could reach it, the servant beside the door made the announcement of another arrival in their midst.

"Sir Oswald Quinn," he called out in a very proper tone.

Mary suppressed a curse as she watched her father enter the room. Part of the agreement Crispin had struck in order to keep her in his home was that invitations to these Upper Ten Thousand events would be extended to her father. As a grasping social climber, Sir Oswald never missed a one.

But she couldn't face him right now when she felt so very raw. She couldn't listen to him mutter about her failure to land a husband or his plans for her if she didn't come out of this Season wed. So she turned away, slipping into the protective veil of the crowd.

She forced a smile to people she knew as she maneuvered through the crush toward the doors which led to the terrace. She would be safe outside, for her father rarely left a ballroom once he entered it, lest he missed an opportunity to lick the boots of someone important.

She turned the handle of the terrace door and stepped outside into the cool night air. As she shut it behind her, she leaned against the barrier briefly and sucked in a few gulping breaths.

"You *will not* cry," she admonished herself softly before she gave her body a little shake and stepped forward to the low wall of the terrace.

She stared down at the garden below. The duke who owned this property had one of the most beautiful gardens in London and its flowers were in full bloom so that the scent of them wafted up on the cool night air.

Somewhere in the trees a nightingale began its song, calling for a mate to join it. Mary frowned, for she had no such easy lure to tempt a companion. Above her, the flutter of wings swooping toward the sound told her the bird had gotten its wish.

She looked down on the garden again with a sigh. "How I wish I were a bird, so I could fly away," she said, not bothering to whisper the words since she was alone on the terrace.

Or at least she'd thought she was. As soon as the words left her lips, there was a rustling sound behind her. She spun around to watch the dark outline of a man rise from a table that had been hidden in the shadow of the house. She couldn't make out his features, but his voice was very deep and rough as he said, "Miss, if you intend to jump, I hope you'll reconsider. I don't want to have to stop you."

Edward could see that the young woman standing frighteningly close to the terrace wall was startled by his sudden appearance, and he supposed that was his own fault. He'd watched her depart the house, realized she didn't see him there in the dark, and had fully intended to simply allow her to believe she was alone. He didn't want to be disturbed, no matter how fetching she was. And she was damned fetching, indeed.

But he had other things to consider at present beyond her slender frame, her oval face with its high cheekbones, her full lips.

"You scared me nearly to death!" she gasped as she threw a hand to her chest, drawing his attention, of course, to her small but rather perfect breasts.

He moved toward her into the light so she could see he wasn't quite an ogre, at least not in appearance. "As you did me, miss."

He frowned as images from the past came rushing back over him. He made a concerted effort to shove them aside.

Her lips pinched as she looked over her shoulder at the terrace wall edge. "I had no intention of jumping, sir, I assure you."

"Good," he drawled, unable to take his eyes off of her now that the moonlight made it easier for him to see the details of her face. Her eyes were a fetching green-gray, pale in comparison to her dark hair.

"Who are you?" she asked, tilting her head as if she were examining him just as closely as he was her.

He cleared his throat. It really had been a long time since he was out in Society if he couldn't keep basic courtesy at the forefront of his mind.

"Er, I'm sorry," he stammered. "I am the Marquis of Woodley."

"Miss Mary Quinn, my lord," she said, holding out a gloved hand. He hesitated, but then took it, shaking gently. Even through the barriers of cloth separating them, her hands were warm, and touching her sent a strange shock of awareness through him. "Do you often sit in the dark spying on potential jumpers? Is it a vocation or a hobby?"

To his surprise, he felt a smile turn up his lips. It was a very odd sensation, for he hadn't performed the expression in what seemed like years. She was a cheeky little thing as well as pretty, and he found he liked the combination.

"I only perform this duty on the third Saturday of each month," he retorted, surprised he could find such a teasing response.

She laughed, the sound as fine as the nightingale's song had been. "You must check your calendar, my lord. Tonight is not the third Saturday of the month."

He shook his head. "Damn. I will have to find something else to do, then."

He wished he could take the words back the moment he said them. They were flirtatious, and he wasn't certain that was a particularly good idea. Oh, he needed to find a lady to court, it was why he was back out in Society after so many years hiding away, but he hadn't intended to embark upon that course of action by dallying with a stranger on a terrace.

But Mary didn't seem to sense his discomfort, for she only laughed again, her face bright and open in the moonlight. With a frown, he paced away to the wall behind her and looked down into the gardens as she had been doing. From these dizzying heights, being a bird and flying away as she had said didn't seem like the worst idea.

She stopped laughing as he moved away, and cleared her throat with discomfort. "So, do you mind me asking what your *real* reason for being out here is?"

He turned to face her with a shrug. "Have you been in there?" he asked, motioning to the ballroom behind the glass terrace doors, even though he knew that was exactly where she had come from.

She nodded.

"*That* is why I'm out here."

He expected her to further question him or try to coax him back into the throng like most young women would do. Instead, she let out a heavy sigh. "I cannot blame you, then."

He arched a brow in surprise. "A pretty girl like you, want to avoid a ball? You must thrive in there." She let out a bark of laughter that was anything but joyous, and his frown deepened. "So you aren't enjoying yourself?"

She shook her head. "It is difficult to enjoy oneself when all of one's friends are recently and deliriously happily married. And if that wasn't enough, don't forget that one's father is likely considering selling one to some hundred-year-old earl so that he can cash in on a titled man's fortune and influence."

Edward drew back at her unexpected honesty and the pain which accompanied it. "Miss Quinn—"

She blushed from the roots of her hair to the neckline of her gown. "I'm sorry, that was far too direct. I should not dump my troubles onto a poor stranger who was only coming out here to escape silly girls just like me."

She moved as if to return to the ballroom and he caught her hand, holding her in place. She pivoted back to stare up at him, her full lips parted slightly in surprise.

"Not at all," he said, his voice rough with desire he was surprised and dismayed to feel as he stared down at her.

"I-I should go back inside," she stammered, but did not remove her hand from his grasp. "I will be missed."

"Of course you will. Would you mind if I escort you back in? Perhaps claim the next open dance on your card?"

She hesitated for a fraction of a moment as her gaze slowly moved over his face. Then she nodded. "It seems the very next one is open, my lord. I would very much like to share it with you."

There was an odd sensation in Edward's chest as he glided

Mary's hand into the crook of his arm and led her to the ballroom. He had felt that feeling before. He'd promised himself it would never be repeated. So as they moved onto the dance floor, seemingly all eyes in the party on them, he steeled his throbbing heart and forced himself to be all propriety as the music began.

She smiled up at him after a few turns of the dance had passed, challenging his resolve almost immediately. "You know, I have just realized I have not seen you at one of these events before, my lord."

He gritted his teeth at the question that was not a question. As she spun elegantly, he tried to find a response. "I have been much needed elsewhere," he said.

She tilted her head. "That sounds very covert, my lord. More spying on terraces?"

He couldn't help the smile that betrayed him, even though the subject she'd struck upon gave him so little pleasure. "Something like that."

"Well, I'm glad you came out tonight," she said as the music ended and she executed a slight curtsey. "It made an unbearable evening much more pleasant in the end."

He hesitated, longing to reach out and place a hand on her arm again. Wanting to take her back out to the terrace and simply talk to her. Perhaps even steal a kiss.

But instead, he took a long step back and issued a stiff bow. "I'm pleased to be of service. Good night, Miss Quinn."

Then he turned and all but ran from the ballroom, ran from her and the strange attraction between them that was immediate and dangerous. He didn't look back even as he felt her stare on his retreating back with every step. And he didn't breathe again until he was safe in the foyer, waiting for his carriage to be brought to take him home.

"That was so very strange," he muttered as he watched his rig pull up to retrieve him. "And it must never again be repeated."

CHAPTER TWO

Mary rested her head back against the carriage seat and her eyes fluttered shut. It had been a very long night, after all, and she could not wait to fall into her waiting bed. Not that she was certain sleep would come. She had a great deal on her mind, including the odd and interesting Lord Woodley, who had teased her, attracted her and then run from her not two hours before.

She felt her sister and brother-in-law watching her from across the carriage and opened one eye. Their arms were interlinked, as always, physical proof of their powerful love for each other. Even the birth of their first child—a daughter, Esmeralda—had not diminished their connection, but seem to make it bloom all the more beautifully. Despite all that, Crispin's attention was now focused firmly and unwaveringly on Mary's face.

She straightened. "What is it? You look very serious, Crispin, and you never look serious."

Mary expected him to smile. He always indulged her cheeky teasing of him and was a good sport. But tonight his frown remained.

"It isn't our father, is it?" she asked, her gaze flitting to her sister. "Gemma, he isn't stealing me back yet! The Season isn't over and I cannot—"

Gemma reached out across the distance between them and

took her hand. "Mary, calm yourself. The bargain Crispin and Rafe made with our father to keep you in our care remains in place."

Crispin's expression softened. "I swear to you, Mary, I am working very hard to insure you remain with us permanently. I'll move heaven and earth if I have to. You don't need to worry yourself."

Mary sagged in relief, though she couldn't do anything *but* worry as her uncertain future loomed before her. "Well, if isn't the less-than-illustrious Sir Oswald Quinn who makes you two look so upset, what is it? Did I do something wrong?"

Crispin seemed to struggle with words before he stammered, "I—we saw you dancing with Woodley tonight."

Mary blinked. It was her brief exchange with the marquis that made Crispin look so serious? The same exchange that had been haunting her own mind since their dance?

"I—yes," she said, still uncertain. Crispin had never seemed very interested in her dance partners beyond asking her if she had enjoyed herself at gatherings. "He is a marquis, you know."

She didn't know why she had added that fact about Woodley to the conversation. Title meant very little to her except that she knew her father wanted her to marry one. Even he couldn't sneeze at a marquis, could he? Not that Woodley had shown any interest in her. Well, he *had*, but then he had darted away so abruptly…

She truly did not understand men.

"Yes," Gemma said. "We know his rank."

Mary wrinkled her brow. "You both look oddly serious about this. What is going on? I merely talked to the man on the terrace for a moment and then shared one sorry little dance with him. I hardly think that warrants these dour expressions."

Gemma worried her lip, and she and Crispin exchanged another meaningful glance. Now Mary leaned in.

"What are you so worried about?" she demanded. "You are starting to frighten me!"

"I'm sorry, Mary." Gemma looked genuinely distressed. "We aren't trying to be frightening."

"When you talked, did Woodley mention anything about me?" Crispin pressed.

Mary was still trying to work out where in the world these questions were coming from as she said, "No, but nor did I. Are you two acquainted?"

Crispin drew in a long breath. "In a way."

His thin lips and pale face made her huff out a breath. "Goodness, this is ridiculous. What is wrong with the man that you two look as though I had gone off to St. Helena, brought Napoleon back with me and danced with *him* at the ball?"

Crispin turned his face, like he didn't want her to see his expression. "There is nothing wrong with him, Mary."

Mary was about to stomp her foot at his reticence when Gemma said, "No, nothing at all. I do not know the man very well, myself, but I have never had a poor interaction with him, nor heard anything untoward about his behavior. It isn't that he is scandalous."

Mary threw up her hands. Didn't they know this wasn't helping? It was only making her even more confused. "Then what is it? For you two have never taken such a strange and intense interest in my dancing with a man. A man, I would add, who left the ball because he apparently found my company so offensive. A man who I will likely never dance with, nor perhaps even see, again."

She said the words and there was a strange disappointment that filled her. She had truly enjoyed the uncharacteristic banter she had felt comfortable sharing with Woodley. Although she had apparently frightened him away with her candor and her teasing, for those few moments she had felt so very comfortable.

But it mattered little. Woodley apparently didn't like her and she truly didn't understand why Crispin and Gemma were so concerned about her dancing with him.

"It is true that you will likely not interact with him again,"

Crispin said slowly. "After all, he rarely comes out into Society."

"He may be returning," Gemma said softly. "Even after...*everything*, he must be in want of a wife to carry on the title."

Crispin's lips thinned again. "That is true."

Mary sighed heavily. "You are both very confusing and I am becoming upset with your odd behavior. Will you tell me what is going on?"

Gemma shook her head. "Nothing, dearest. We had some small anxiety that you had met Woodley, but if you say that the two of you did not suit, then any concerns we had are not to be dealt with. Now, did you see Lady Anne's purple gown?"

Mary frowned. Gemma was trying to distract her with talk of dresses, even though she could read some lingering concerns in her sister's stare. And though it should have made her think less of Woodley that her sister and brother-in-law had such hesitations about him, it made the already fascinating marquis even more interesting to her.

It was really too bad they would likely never meet again.

Edward shifted uncomfortably as he balanced his plate of little finger sandwiches in what suddenly felt like his huge hand. God, he had forgotten how awful these Society events were, whether a ball or a garden party like this one. When he first entered Society, he didn't remember being so uncomfortable.

Of course, that had all been before. Before...everything.

"You look like you want to run."

Edward jolted and turned to find his youngest sister Audrey had sidled up beside him. At twenty-four years of age, she was unmarried and their mother had insisted he escort her to a few events this Season. But everyone in the family knew that Audrey was actually chaperoning him, bringing him back into the Society he so wished to avoid.

He frowned. "Is running an option?"

"No, I am afraid not." She let out a sigh. "But you cannot be unhappy, can you? You have a plate of cucumber sandwiches."

He held the plate out. "Have them, Audrey."

She took it with a laugh. "This *is* dire if you cannot eat. You have never had that affliction."

His mouth turned down even further. "Once I did."

His sister's laughter faded. "Edward…oh, Edward, I'm sorry, I didn't mean to—"

He cut her off with a wave of his hand. "It isn't your fault. I don't want to be here and I am merely being maudlin."

Audrey squeezed his arm gently. "Is there *anything* here to tempt you?"

He looked around and suddenly everything in the garden seemed to come to a screeching halt. There amongst the trimmed rose bushes was a far more interesting and beautiful flower. Miss Mary Quinn was standing with another lady, he didn't know her name. Mary laughed as they talked, her animated face lit up with pleasure about whatever the subject of their interaction was.

He had not seen her for three days, not since his humiliating retreat after their dance. And yet she had been all he had thought about during that time. He had even awoken in his bed, sweating, his cock hard as steel and Mary Quinn's name a moan on his lips.

What the hell was wrong with him?

"Edward?" Audrey repeated, dragging him from his thoughts.

He shook his head. Audrey and Mary would be of an age, he thought, and perhaps his sister knew the other woman. But he didn't want to ask. In part because if he showed any interest in any woman, his family would pounce on that fact like a pack of ravenous dogs. Well-meaning dogs, yes, but dogs nonetheless. And in part because he dared not feed the odd desire he felt toward Mary. In fact, what he *should* do was turn around and walk in the other direction, not alert Mary to his presence.

But instead, he found himself unable to tear his gaze away.

"You know, I think I see a friend across the way," he lied. "To keep you happy and to prove that I am not a hopeless hermit, I will go and speak to him. Excuse me."

Audrey blinked up at him, her face lined with confusion. "Very well. I'll see you later, Edward."

He hardly heard her, so focused was he on the steps that separated him from Mary. Ten paces, fifteen paces...her friend smiled and left her, and now she was alone...twenty paces and he was here, stopping at her side. She started as she turned her face and noticed him, and then that fetching pink blush washed over her pale skin once more.

"Good afternoon, Miss Quinn," he said with what he hoped wasn't an awkward smile. It suddenly felt like a very awkward smile, indeed.

"My lord," she said, dropping her gaze away from his. "I-I didn't realize you were here today."

"My mother insisted I chaperone my youngest sister, Audrey." He motioned behind him, toward his sister.

Mary followed his gaze with wide eyes and then she darted her stare back to him. "You are Lady Audrey's brother?"

He nodded. "I wondered if you two were acquainted. You must be of an age, I think."

Mary smiled, the first smile she had gifted him with since his approach. "I only know her a little, I'm afraid, but I've always liked her."

"Yet another thing we have in common, for I have always liked her, too," he teased, but even as he said the words, he marveled at them. When had he last felt so *light*? He truly could not recall.

She laughed, filling the air around them with music and

drawing attention from several of those close by. He felt their stares on him, felt their judgments, and his cravat suddenly seemed too tight.

"Are you well?" Mary asked, her laughter fading.

His eyes widened. "I—why do you ask?"

She shrugged. "You suddenly grew pale. You aren't planning to run away again, are you?"

"The idea does appeal," he admitted. "Though not away from you." He cleared his throat. He was about to do something that he would likely regret. "Would you like to take a walk with me?"

She didn't respond, but instead suddenly shifted her focus to a spot behind him. He turned and followed her glance and found a fat, older, red-faced man toddling down the stairs toward the garden.

"Oh, yes, please, let's walk," she said. "*Now*, if you don't mind."

He wrinkled his brow but did not question her. He took her arm and guided her through the garden, past the people, through the maze of rose bushes, down the pretty path and into a maze of shrubbery trimmed to look like various odd animals. The sound of the crowd transformed to a faint buzz behind them, and at the same moment they let out twin sighs of relief.

He looked at her and smiled as he motioned to a bench in the midst of the shrubbery animals, and she nodded as they sat together.

"It seems we have the same affliction, since we both want to run from the crowd," he said.

She tilted her head slightly, examining him more closely. "Do you mind if I ask you a question?"

He nodded. "Of course not."

"That night at the ball, did you leave because I did something wrong?"

He drew back in horror. "No, no, of course not, Mary!"

She blinked at his use of her given name, but he did not correct his social faux pas. He rather liked the feel of her name on his tongue. It was likely as close as he'd get to tasting her skin, feeling her kiss.

"Then why *did* you all but bolt?"

He shifted. "You are direct."

Her smile flickered. "So I am told, especially by my brother-in-law."

He hesitated. Did he really want to confess to this young woman? A part of him truly did, but he couldn't go too far.

"I-I have not been in Society for many years," he admitted slowly. "For reasons I do not wish to discuss, though I'm certain you could find out some of the details if you ask the right people." He pushed aside the bitterness that went with that sentence and tried to continue. "Being in the crush, feeling the weight of expectation, well, it is not easy for me. It was cowardly to run that night, and if it left you feeling you had done something wrong, for that I am truly sorry, Mary."

She shook her head. "You needn't apologize, though I am happy it wasn't me that made you dart from the ball. I do understand the pressures of Society. I often wish I could escape, myself."

He nodded. "Yes, after all, I found you on the terrace that night, didn't I? Wishing you could fly away like the nightingale?"

She blushed, but it was her only response.

He continued carefully. "You told me then something about the happy marriages of your friends and family and the bad intentions of your father." She nodded. "Was that him on the steps up at the house? I ask because that man's arrival seemed to make you intent on escape."

Her lips parted in surprise and then she ducked her head. "I said too much that first night, my lord."

"Edward," he corrected softly. "If we are to be friends and share such confidences, should we not be on a first name basis?"

She hesitated a moment. "Edward, I do not wish to burden you with my petty complaints."

"Even if I offer to carry them a moment?" he pressed. He found himself leaning in and caught a whiff of the soft, peachy scent of her pale skin. God, he wanted to taste her.

Her breath came shorter as she whispered, "It is all a little too humiliating."

He felt his hand move, watched it like it was disconnected from his body and mind. His fingers brushed the satin of her cheek, glided up until he cupped her face in a far too familiar way.

"Mary," he whispered. "It is just you and me."

"Yes," she breathed. "It is."

He couldn't resist. He lowered his face to hers and suddenly his lips were brushing across hers. She lifted to meet him, her eagerness a lure he couldn't deny. Suddenly what had been chaste and gentle turned heated. He darted his tongue out and she opened for him, gasping as he delved in to taste her. She made a soft whimper, a tiny sound of surprise and surrender mixed, and his whole body went hard and ready.

He wanted her. It was a shocking truth. He wanted to drop to his knees and lift her skirts and pleasure her. He wanted to feel her body pulse around him and let her milk him to completion. He wanted to strip her bare and look into her eyes as she gave him everything she was.

But those thoughts were too much, too shocking, so instead he forced himself to abruptly break the kiss and get to his feet.

CHAPTER THREE

Mary gasped for air as she watched Woodley...*Edward* walk away from her. He had kissed her. Truly kissed her, the same way she sometimes caught Crispin kissing Gemma. A kiss filled with passion and desire, and her body felt like it was on fire as a result.

"I'm sorry," he said without looking at her, his shoulders lifting and falling on ragged breaths that were much like her own. "I should not have done that."

She got to her own feet, heat burning her cheeks. "Wh-why?"

When he faced her again, he was expressionless. "It wasn't proper."

She nodded. Of course he was right. That was the kind of kiss that got women into trouble. The kind which led to ruin and scandal and even forced marriages. And yet Edward's dismissal of her, even couched in terms of her own protection, stung.

He cleared his throat. "Despite my very bad behavior, I *do* want to know why you fear your father, why you think he is bound to sell you off to an unwanted suitor," he said, remaining at least three paces away from her.

She turned away. It seemed more intimate to confess the truth than it had for his hot, slick tongue to breach her mouth and taste her so sweetly. Certainly the second was far more enjoyable than the first. She found herself answering regardless.

"He forced my sister into both her first and second marriages for his own gain," she said, her voice shaking. "She is very happy now, but that was a turn of fate rather than by his design. He wants to be associated with a title, and since I have failed him for four Seasons, he claims he will retake control of me from my sister's care at the end of this one."

Edward's mouth pinched with displeasure. "Why haven't you been successful?"

She jerked her gaze to him. "I-I—" she stammered, and once again found the truth falling from her lips. Edward inspired that, it seemed. "My sister and I have said that it is because our father inserts himself whenever there is an interested party. He is humiliatingly obvious in his drive for social increase and it has scared away more than one man. But it is more than that. I have not found a husband because…"

"Because?" he encouraged when she cut herself off.

"Because I want to love someone," she whispered. "I want to be loved in return. I want someone to kiss me as my sister's husband always kisses her." She blushed. "It is the way you just kissed me, actually. Like you couldn't get close enough. Like you wanted me with every fiber of your being."

He froze in his place, staring at her. She couldn't read his expression. Did he think her an utter idiot? That was how she felt at present.

"Or perhaps I misunderstood your desires when you kissed me," she murmured.

The three paces between them vanished so quickly that when Edward reached her, she started in surprise. He caught her arm to keep her from walking away and dragged her closer, until she molded against him in scandalous closeness.

"You misunderstand nothing." His voice was rough before his mouth descended on hers a second time.

She knew in her heart that she should push him away. After all, his statement that what they were doing was improper was correct, and she was on shaky enough ground when it came to her future. But as his hot lips burned against hers, as his tongue gently traced the crease of her mouth and then past it, she forgot all that. She forgot everything except him. Him and how he made her aching body feel.

She had never been so aware of her skin. All over, even beneath her gown, she tingled. Those tingles seemed to focus in the most improper of places. Her nipples, for example, and between her legs where the tingle transformed to a throbbing ache she longed to ease.

His arms came around her, imprisoning her in his heat, and she sighed as she relaxed against him. They staggered back and he found the bench they had abandoned earlier. He sank onto the stone and dragged her onto his lap where he continued to explore her mouth with thorough kisses.

And then her mouth ceased to be enough and he pressed those hot, wonderful lips to her neck.

"Edward," she sighed, tilting her head back and allowing him access. God, the things he did to her. It was like being awakened from a lifelong sleep and suddenly her body felt foreign and funny.

"Do you know how long it's been since I wanted someone this badly?" he grunted between sweeping his lips back and forth on her throat.

She shook her head because she wasn't certain she could form coherent words beyond moaning of his name.

He drew back and looked down at her in his lap. "Too long. I didn't think I would ever want someone again, Mary. But you are so sweet. And even though I know it's wrong, I want to do such wicked things to you."

Her eyes went wide. Wicked things. That sounded both terrifying and oh-so-promising. She licked her suddenly dry lips and he grunted out a pained sound. "What kind of wicked things?"

"I want to kiss every inch of your body. I want to claim you. I want to awaken you to all the desires you don't even know you have. I want to watch you quake in anticipation for hours while I keep you on the edge of pleasure and then take you over with the flick of my wrist. I want you to know you're mine. And none of that makes any sense because you are almost a stranger to me."

She stared at him, shocked by his words and he frowned.

"You must hate me for being so forward," he said.

She cupped his cheeks and looked into his eyes. Beautiful dark brown eyes that sparked with swirling desires much more powerful than she could understand. But also eyes that spoke of great sadness.

"I don't hate you," she reassured him softly. "I felt a draw to you from the moment you stood up from the shadows and nearly frightened me to death. And now that you've touched me, I am drawn to these acts you describe even if propriety tells me I should recoil."

His hand moved to cup the back of her head and he made a guttural, possessive sound deep within his throat before his mouth covered hers yet again. She arched into him, aching for more, not understanding quite what the more was, but needing it nonetheless.

She would have surrendered to him in that moment. The fact that it was midafternoon in the middle of a stranger's garden be damned. She would have given him whatever he asked for in her tangled, confused, wanton state. But she never had to make that desperate decision. As he shifted her in his lap, deepening the kiss to what even she recognized was a point of no return, there was a sound behind her that froze time, that stopped her heart, that made all the beauty of this moment shatter into pieces.

It was the sound of her father's smug voice.

"Well, well, well," he said, and Edward immediately broke the kiss and leapt up, forcing Mary to her feet as well.

Edward steadied her as they turned to face the intruder and Mary covered her face as she realized Sir Oswald was not alone. Right behind him were a desperately pale Gemma and a very angry-looking Crispin.

Her father laughed. "It looks like Miss Mary has taken care of her husband problem all on her own at last."

Gemma's father was talking, but Edward heard none of it. All he could do was stare at the man's companions. He knew Crispin and Gemma Flynn all too well. The two men shared a sordid history.

"Woodley!" Flynn growled, taking a step forward that was only stopped by his wife grasping his arm with both hands and holding him steady.

"Crispin, no," she said, casting a glance behind her toward the house and the party buzzing not so far away. "Don't make my sister's troubles worse."

Edward's mouth dropped open and he stared from Mary to Gemma and back again. The two women *did* share some small features now that he made the connection, but he had never guessed that Mary's sister was this woman. *This* woman of all women, married to this man of all men.

"Gemma Flynn is your sister?" he asked, interrupting Mary's father's tirade.

Mary turned her impossibly lovely face toward his. She was almost deathly pale, the bright, bubbling vitality of her eyes dulled by pain and embarrassment.

"*That* is what you want to know when my father is insisting we wed?"

He blinked. Was that what the man had been saying? He turned his attention toward her father. "See here...er..."

The heavyset man stepped forward, hand outstretched and face bright with joy, far from the anger he should have exhibited upon finding his innocent daughter in such a state with a man.

"Sir Oswald Quinn at your service, my lord. And indeed, I

was just saying that the only thing you two can do after being caught in such a position is to wed. Quickly."

There was a steel in Sir Oswald's eyes that Edward stepped away from. The man looked like a cat that had cornered a wounded bird and now intended to play with it.

"Papa!" Mary burst out, panic in her tone. "Stop this at once."

Her sister took her hand and drew her gently away from Edward. He was surprised at just how much he wanted to take her opposite hand and bring her back.

"Yes, stop it, Father," Gemma said, her voice much stronger than Mary's. "You will *not* force anyone into anything. Not while I have breath in my body."

"What the hell are you doing, Woodley?" Flynn asked through obviously clenched teeth. "Seducing young women in a garden at two in the afternoon? Is that how you exit your hermitage or is it because Mary is related to *me*? Exacting your revenge at last, are we?"

Edward flinched at the accusation and the memories it brought back. His pain was made worse by the expression of confusion that flitted over Mary's face. She shook off her sister's hand and stared at him.

"What are you talking about? *Do* you two know each other?"

"It's a long story," Flynn growled.

Mary huffed out her breath. "Not too long if it involves me! Tell me at once."

"Please, there is no time!" Gemma shook her head and glanced over her shoulder again.

Edward saw the same thing as she did. Their raised voices had begun to attract attention from the party above and people were coming down the path to investigate. It was one thing to be caught in a scandalous position by Mary's family, but quite another to be overrun by the cream of the *ton*. That would not end well.

"Perhaps we should all calm ourselves and return to the

party," Edward suggested. "We could reconvene at another time at my estate or the Flynns' and discuss this matter in private where Mary's reputation will not be further damaged."

To his surprise, Sir Oswald laughed. "I don't think so. When they arrive, I intend to tell them exactly what I stumbled upon. I will call you out to duel in the morning if you do not agree to make her your bride."

Gemma shoved Mary behind her with a gasp of pure pain and this time didn't stop Flynn when he lunged at Sir Oswald. Flynn grabbed his father-in-law's lapels and shook him hard.

"Mind yourself, you reaching, piggish bastard."

Sir Oswald's eyes were lit with fear, but as he glanced up toward the approaching voices, he still smiled. "Make it worse, Flynn. Please. It will only make the gossip louder."

Flynn's face was red and angry, but he slowly released his father-in-law and shoved him aside hard enough that Sir Oswald nearly fell to the dirt.

Then Flynn turned on Edward again. "You never answered my question. Is this your attempt at vengeance?"

Edward swallowed hard. "Had I known Mary was in any way related to you, I never would have spoken to her, let alone kissed her."

Behind Gemma, Mary gasped and he flinched at the tears that filled her eyes. She turned her face and stared at the ground at her feet, her spirit obviously bruised. And he wished he could take the words back. He wished he could change so much about this situation.

"So you didn't know," Flynn said with what sounded like relief. "That is something. But you *have* compromised her. Or at least her father will make sure that is what the *ton* believes. So what do we do now?"

Edward stared at Mary. Even though she wouldn't meet his eyes, he knew she wanted him. She might feel differently in the future, once she had heard the whole sordid story that had kept him hidden from Society, that had destroyed him, that had damaged his family, perhaps beyond repair.

But could he damage her so cavalierly by walking away now?

He knew he couldn't. So he cleared his throat and said bizarre words that felt like a dream and a nightmare at the same time.

"*We* will do nothing," he said. "*I* will marry her."

Mary came around her sister with a second gasp, this one of surprise rather than pain or embarrassment. "Marry me?" she repeated, eyes wide and hands shaking. "But you just told Crispin that you don't even want me."

He shook his head. "Is that what you heard?" He moved toward her. "Mary, I never said I didn't want you. Soon you will have everything explained and then you'll understand why I told Flynn that I would have avoided you had I known your relationship to him. But it never, ever would have been because I didn't want you. I think I proved that by putting us in this untenable position here in the garden."

Her lips parted as if she wanted to say more, but before she could, the crowd from above descended into the maze.

"Is something going on?" said Lord Faleford, the owner of the home where they were gathered. "We heard shouting."

Sir Oswald stepped forward with that cat-like grin on his face again. The one Edward sorely wanted to smack away, considering how mercenary and cruel the man was.

"It is happy news, my lords and ladies," he said, addressing the crowd like a barker at the circus. "My daughter Mary has just agreed to marry the Marquis of Woodley."

Edward squeezed his eyes shut briefly as the crowd rumbled in surprise and shock. That was it. His future was set. He opened his eyes a second time to find his sister Audrey pushing her way to the front of the groups. She was suddenly pale and her pretty face was filled with questions Edward knew would be repeated by his entire family far too soon.

He turned his face from hers and instead reached out to take Mary's hand. He drew her to his side with a small smile of what he hoped would be comfort and said, "What Sir Oswald says is true. Mary has agreed to make me the happiest of men."

There was a pause and then there was polite clapping from the crowd. Lord Faleford turned toward them. "I think this calls for champagne. Come!"

The main group followed him, joined by a beaming and boasting Sir Oswald, as he headed back through the garden to the house, but Gemma, Flynn and Audrey stayed back with Mary and Edward.

"Edward?" his sister whispered. "What is going on?"

He drew Mary forward gently. "Audrey, I believe you know Miss Quinn a little."

Audrey nodded to Mary. "A little. But you two are engaged? Marrying?"

Mary ducked her head again. "It is sudden."

"I would say so," Audrey agreed, continuing to search his face.

He forced a wider smile. "Be happy for me, sister. This is a banner day."

Audrey held his stare and he knew she was thinking about his past. About their fractured family which had been caused by more than one ill-conceived union. He waited with bated breath to see how she would respond to this news.

To his relief, she took Mary's hand. "Welcome to our family, Miss Quinn. *Mary*."

Mary lifted her gaze with a weak smile. "Thank you," she whispered.

Gemma moved forward, pale and grim. "We should go up before we are missed."

"There is more to discuss," Flynn said through clenched teeth.

His wife nodded as she slipped a hand through the crook of his arm. "Yes. And we will discuss it. Later. When we can do it in privacy."

Edward turned on him. "Your wife is right, Flynn. As usual. Come, let us go up and join the others. I swear to you that when this is over, you may rail at me for as long and as cruelly as you like."

Flynn leaned in as they began to walk. "I certainly intend to."

Usually that would have angered Edward. Seeing Flynn normally brought back the worst of memories. But today, as he looked down at his now-bride-to-be, he pushed all that aside. He had made this bed. And he couldn't say he didn't look forward to certain parts of lying in it.

CHAPTER FOUR

Mary paced the parlor and wrung her hands. Outside, the dusky night settled over London, but she hardly noticed the gathering dark. Not when so much was unresolved inside. She glanced at the clock.

"Do you think he will come?" she asked, hating to have to voice the question out loud.

Gemma sat on the settee, baby Esmeralda smiling and cooing in her arms, but her face remained drawn and anxious after the afternoon's goings on. Crispin stood at the fireplace, watching the flames with anger pulling his mouth down.

"I'm certain he will," Gemma said softly, casting a quick glance at her husband. "Woodley's family must have had questions about his sudden engagement when he returned his sister to their mother's home."

"Woodley may be many things," Crispin said without taking his eyes from the fire. "But he *will* come."

Mary should have taken solace in their words, but since she was so utterly in the dark about the past that seemed to bind her brother-in-law, her sister and her now-intended, she couldn't.

"Father set this up, I think," she said instead of facing the truth.

Gemma frowned. "Why do you say that?"

She shook her head before she explained the theory that

had been troubling her for hours. "The other night when I danced with Woodley, I *know* he saw us. And today when he entered the garden, his gaze moved to us, too. Woodley was too much of a draw for Sir Oswald to resist. Titled? Money? He was the perfect catch. When Edward and I went for our walk, he must have followed, hoping to catch us in a tenuous position."

"Or to create one if he didn't," Crispin growled. "I would put *nothing* past that man."

Mary moved toward him. In the two years he and her sister had been wed, she had come to truly care for Crispin and see him as her own brother. To now have him so angry at her hurt.

"At least you will no longer have to have me intruding upon your household," she offered. "Failing in every attempt to land a husband in traditional means."

Crispin's angry expression softened as he jerked his gaze to her. Without hesitation, he moved forward and caught both her hands. "Mary, you cannot believe I have *ever* regretted having you here or have been disappointed in you in any way."

She blinked at tears that suddenly flooded her eyes. "I cannot help but be disappointed in myself. I could only trick a man into marrying me, not tempt him, even with the help of you and your family."

Crispin squeezed her hands a little tighter. "Lovely Mary, you tempted this man all on your own. Your father chose to trade on that slip of propriety and that angers me because we wanted you to be autonomous in your choices. But my disgust is aimed at Sir Oswald, never you. I adore you and you shall never believe otherwise, is that clear?"

Mary smiled as he swiped a tear from her cheek. "Yes, Crispin. Very clear."

Gemma stood and moved toward them. Crispin held out his arms for the baby and Gemma passed her off and slipped an arm around Mary. "Do you like him?"

Mary saw her sister's concern in her eyes and could not

blame her. Gemma had been forced by their father into a union when she was young, and it had not been a happy time. Her marriage to Crispin had begun much the same way, though it was now so loving and perfect that no one could speak of it without smiling.

But Gemma knew the potential pain a forced future could bring, better than anyone.

"I *do* like him," Mary reassured her. "From the first moment I met him, I liked him very much. My hesitations are that we are forced into this course so swiftly and that he obviously shares a past with Crispin. Won't you tell me now what that past is?"

Crispin and Gemma exchanged a glance, but before they could speak, their butler appeared in the doorway. "Lord Woodley," he announced.

Mary stepped away from her sister, toward the tall and oh-so-handsome man who stepped through the door. Her fiancé. He had a very grim expression.

"I would rather be the one to tell you the details of my past," he said, obviously referring to the question she had asked a moment ago. He glanced at Crispin and Gemma. "And I would like to do it alone."

Crispin moved forward, somehow still managing to look intimidating even with Esmeralda perched on his hip. "You will do no such thing. Leaving you two alone would be most improper considering what happened this afternoon."

Mary waited for her sister to agree, to be thwarted in this moment that felt so very private between her and her intended. But instead, Gemma touched Crispin's shoulder gently.

"Let them be, Crispin. It is Woodley's right to tell her this story in his own way. His own time. After all, it isn't really yours, is it? Or mine?"

Crispin hesitated as he stared down at Gemma. Then he nodded. "No, it is not my story any longer, you are right. *You* are my story." He glanced at Edward and his expression was a fraction gentler. "Take your time, Woodley. But know I am just on the other side of that door."

Edward looked as surprised by their acquiescence as Mary felt, but he nodded as Gemma and Crispin left the room. Gemma even closed the door behind her to give them privacy.

Mary stared at the now-shut barrier. They were well and truly alone. And she felt so incredibly awkward at that fact since she had truly no idea how Edward felt or what he thought or even if he blamed her for what had happened.

Of course, there was only one way to find out. She lifted her chin and looked at him. "I can only imagine what you think of me at present."

His brow wrinkled. "What I think of *you*?"

She shrugged, determined to remain strong even though her insides quaked uncontrollably. "Yes. I allowed you some liberties like the worst wanton, then my father comes along and entraps you, forcing your hand."

"You believe I blame you for my own lack of control and the mercenary qualities of your father?" he asked softly.

"I don't know. I think no one would blame you or your family if you did."

He sighed. "Mary, my family is slightly confused by this news, yes. After all, I left the house with my sister as a single man being harangued to wed. I came home engaged under trying circumstances. But neither they, nor I, judge you for my own lack of control or the circumstances that followed."

"But the scandal—" she began.

He barked out a pained laugh. "I have created worse for them, my dear. And I think that is what you truly want to know, isn't it? You asked Flynn about our shared past?"

Suddenly Mary's lips felt very dry and she found herself nodding far too slowly. "Yes," she whispered.

"My understanding is that before your sister's marriage, you were out in Society but not necessarily in the highest echelons of the *ton*. Do you know that I was married before?"

She tilted her head. "I—no. I admit I know very little about you."

His smile was tight and small. "That will soon change. Yes, I was married. I am a widower."

Mary searched his face for his feelings on the subject, but his expression was curiously flat and unreadable. "How long ago did you lose her?"

"A little more than three years," he said, his tone softer.

She moved toward him, cautiously feeling out his response. "I am sorry, Edward. It must have been difficult for you."

"She was a suicide," he said, his tone still flat. "Though very few people know that fact thanks to my silence and the machinations of her family."

Mary drew back in horror. "A-a suicide!"

He nodded. "She threw herself down the stairs at my London home. And she killed my unborn child in the process."

Mary couldn't help herself—she reached for him, setting her hand on his. "Oh, Edward!"

He stared at their intertwined fingers but didn't move away. "What you must understand, Mary, is that my wife was not a good person. She was manipulative and cruel. Even her death was her way to lash out at me. And she used Flynn to that end as well."

Mary stared. "Crispin? I—what do you mean?"

"Even before we were wed, Alice, my wife, toyed with him. She let him believe she loved him and attempted to make him her lover even after we were married. He was her tool against me, just as the unborn baby was. Just as her attempt at suicide was. Her writings just before her death made it clear she didn't mean to actually succeed, only to make me miserable."

Mary drew away as his words, all these ugly words and stories, sank into her. "Could someone truly be so...so evil?"

"Evil. That is the word for it. Yes. You may ask Flynn, he knows the truth as painfully as I do. Alice's lies very nearly killed him for a long time. It was only your sister who saved him."

Mary nodded. "When they were first forced to wed, I know he was troubled, but I had no idea the cause. He and Gemma are so very happy now."

He pressed his lips together and his tone was bitter. "I had no one like your sister to save me. I retreated after Alice's death. I hid from her family's hatred and my own family's attempts at solace because I didn't want to burden them with the whole truth."

"So they don't know?" Mary said in surprise.

"I told my man of affairs the truth, but not my family," he said, his eyes growing sad. "Shutting them out had consequences because they didn't understand the cause of my grief. I was so lost in betrayal and anger that I couldn't be there to protect my sister. Not Audrey—the older of the two, Claire. She ran away with a charlatan over a year ago and hasn't been seen since. I know they blame me for that. My relationship with my two brothers is strained. I am a broken, ugly man, Mary. *That* is the truth of my past. And now you know it and why it is true. The question is, does it change what you think of me?"

Edward held his breath as he awaited Mary's answer to his question. He knew his voice sounded reasonably calm. After so many years living with his past, he had found ways to control his emotional response to it. But inside, he was desperate.

Mary stared at him, her eyes wide and filled with tears, her lip quivering with emotion. But he couldn't tell how much of what she felt was empathy for him versus anguish for herself that she had become entrapped in such madness merely because he could not control himself.

She cleared her throat. "It *does* change what I think of you, of course," she said softly.

He dipped his head. "I understand your feelings. I don't

know how we will manage to escape this trap your father has placed us in, but I'm sure Flynn and your sister will help us. He, after all, cannot be any happier about this potential union than you now are."

She moved forward, her lips parted, as he spoke. "Edward—Edward, please stop." He ceased speaking at once, pinching his lips together, and waited for her to continue. "When I say my thoughts about you have changed, I do not mean I think less of you. I certainly don't mean that I won't marry you as we agreed."

"No?" The word was said softly because he could hardly speak at all.

Her shaking hand lifted to gently caress his cheek. It took all his self-control to force himself to listen to her next words rather than simply melt into that warm and welcoming touch.

"No," she whispered. "I admit, I'm shocked to hear about your past, both with your wife and what you have shared with my brother-in-law, but it has obviously given you strength rather than weakened you. I admire that you have handled your wife's cruelty and betrayal with such calm. It must have hurt you terribly."

Edward hesitated. So many people close to him had said something similar in the face of grief they couldn't fully grasp. He had always put them off with false smiles and platitudes. But now, staring down into the green-gray of this woman's bright eyes, he couldn't do that. He jerked out a nod.

"What she did broke everything in me, heart and soul," he croaked.

She made a sound of pain in her throat and stroked those soft fingers across his cheek. "Of course it did. But Edward, I want you to know, I am not like *that woman*. Not at all. I would never manipulate you. I would never lie to you or betray you. I would certainly never make a purposeful attempt to hurt you. If we marry...*when* we marry...I will be a good wife to you."

He stared at her. His confession had been for the purpose

of allowing her understanding of his past. It was meant to cut off the possibility that someone else would whisper a twisted version of the tale to her and make her fear or hate him. He had never expected it to elicit a vow of fidelity from Mary.

But hearing it, seeing the earnestness in her eyes as she spoke it...a small part of his heart, a part he had thought long ago murdered by Alice and her lies...sprung back to life.

"I believe you," he whispered, and was rewarded by her beautiful smile again. "And I vow the same to you. This may not be a beginning we expected, Mary, but our life together could be, *will* be, as happy as I can make it."

She lifted her other hand and cupped his face gently. "Edward," she whispered, her voice filled with a need he recognized and mirrored.

"Mary," he returned before he lowered his mouth to hers.

She tasted just as sweet as she had in the garden a few hours before and her moan of surrender was just as wanton and wonderful. Her arms slid around his neck and she lifted against him, as if she couldn't get close enough. He cupped the back of her head with one hand, angling for access, and molded her closer with the other. His erection throbbed, begging him to strip away both her propriety and his own and claim what was his. Now.

Instead, he forced himself to disengage from her, stepping back with a groan.

"If we do not stop this, we will be in much bigger trouble than we already are," he murmured.

Mary was breathing heavily. "I think I'd like to get into trouble."

He scrubbed a hand over his face with another moan. "Great God, the things you say and do to me. But if Flynn catches me with you in my arms, I fear you will not have a bridegroom."

She stepped closer, a wicked light in her eyes. "Isn't it a risk you're willing to take?"

He was about to grasp her hand, drag her against him a

second time when there was a light knock at the door. It opened to reveal Gemma, this time without the baby in tow, and an anxious-looking Crispin. As they entered, Mary sent Edward a sidelong glance and laughed.

And with that one light sound, all his doubts about their future, all his worries about what would happen next fled. He might not have chosen this, but looking at Mary he could see that she was the very best thing for him. Her light and her innocence already brightened his day. And he would get to hold her close forever.

"I hope you have explained as best you could," Flynn said, shooting a brief and somewhat worried glance at Mary.

She smiled and moved toward her brother-in-law, her expression toward him as gentle and understanding as it had been toward Edward. "I'm so sorry for what you went through," she said softly. "Both of you." She glanced back at Edward over her shoulder, temptation without even meaning to be. "But I hope you two will try to put the past behind you. We are all going to be family soon."

Edward tensed. He hadn't fully thought that part through, actually. He would be family with Crispin Flynn, a man he had at times hated, occasionally blamed, sometimes felt sorry for and ultimately envied. The two men locked eyes and he could see Flynn's discomfort mirrored his own.

Slowly, Edward stepped forward and extended his hand. "Shall we let the past rest at last?"

Flynn stared at the outstretched hand for a moment, then extended his own. As they shook, Flynn said, "You always got the worst of what Alice had to give. I am sorry for my part in it."

"There is no need to apologize," Edward said with a shrug that was so dismissive of the pain he had held for years. "We both know that."

"Then we shall start over," Flynn mused as he stepped away with a smile that looked as awkward as Edward now felt. He turned now to Mary. "You are truly happy?"

Mary stepped closer to Edward, and he was surprised as she took his hand, making them a duo, a force which would face the future not individually, but together. She glanced up at him, a small smile brightening her face.

"I think we will be," she reassured her brother-in-law and sister.

Edward blinked in surprise. When Mary said those words, he could believe them. He felt her light spirit winding into his own and filling him with thoughts for the future that he had been squashing since Alice destroyed him years ago. Now he had been placed on a very different path and he found he actually looked forward to it. To her. To *them*.

"Because of the unexpected nature of our engagement, I believe it would be prudent to read the banns swiftly," he said.

Gemma exchanged a look with Mary, and both sisters blushed deeply.

"Given time, our father will only make this situation worse," Gemma verified. "So I cannot disagree that the wedding should occur swiftly and as properly as possible."

Edward waited for dread to hit him, but none came and the smile he gave the women was not forced. "Then I will make sure the first notice is posted this week. Will four weeks be enough time for you to prepare?"

Gemma laughed. "In comparison to how both my weddings were done, that sounds like an eternity. We will be ready, my lord, I assure you."

"I should be going," Edward said with a sigh. "When I took Audrey home and my news came out, my family was naturally taken aback and had a great many questions. I should return to them and do my best to answer. Will you escort me out, Mary?"

The smile on her face had faltered slightly, but she nodded as she reached out to take his arm. "Of course."

He nodded his farewells to Gemma and Flynn, and they exited the room together. As the servant went to call for his carriage, he looked down at Mary with an arched brow.

She seemed to sense his question without him having to state it. "Does your family think very little of me?"

He shook his head. "Only my mother was home when I returned Audrey, and she is surprised, not upset," he reassured her. "My sister said some complimentary things about you and my mother is anxious to meet you and introduce you to my brothers. Perhaps you could join me tomorrow afternoon at my mother's home and become acquainted. Your sister and Flynn are welcome as well."

She nodded, though he could see her anxiety remained despite his reassurances. "I would like that a great deal," she said. "I do not think our time is filled."

"Then expect an invitation from my mother to arrive tomorrow morning."

He reached down to smooth his palm across her cheek, meaning it as a comforting gesture, but the physical reaction touching her brought was swift and sudden. A spark of connection flared between them, the heat of desire that had not been quenched in the garden.

"Mary, Mary," he whispered, watching her eyes dilate with desire that was returned and almost as powerful as his own. "Soon we will be able to finish what was begun this afternoon."

She nodded swiftly. "I know. And I look forward to it more than is proper."

He swallowed at her honest response and his unexpectedly heated reaction. He hadn't wanted another woman like he did this woman for a very, very long time. But now that his desires were awake, he was finding it nearly impossible to deny them.

He dipped his head and kissed her, driving his tongue between her lips, feeling her softness against him with a keenness that walked the line between pleasure and pain. She made a little whimper, a sound of pleasure and surrender, and he nearly came undone right then and there. It was only the smallest part of him that maintained composure, the forced him to release her and step away, his breath short.

They stared at each other for a charged moment, and then the rumbling of his carriage on the drive as it pulled to a stop and waited for him broke the moment. He smiled.

"I'm glad we're reading the banns immediately," he said, and was surprised to discover that it was utterly the truth.

She smiled. "Good day, my lord. I'll see you tomorrow."

He gave a small bow and darted out the door, his step too light for a man who had been trapped into a marriage that day. But as he settled into the carriage and it began to drive away, he realized it was because he didn't feel trapped after all. He felt like he was being saved.

CHAPTER FIVE

Edward took a long, deep breath before he walked up the marble stairs to the front door of his mother's home. It had been less than twenty-four hours since his last appearance here, but it felt like a lifetime.

The door opened and his mother's butler appeared, looking serious as ever.

"Welcome back, Lord Woodley," he intoned as he stepped back to allow Edward entry into the foyer.

"Thank you, Vernon," he said with another sigh. "I assume they are all gathered in the west parlor?"

The servant nodded. "Shall I announce you?"

"No need. I'm sure they're standing by like jackals about to pounce," he said with a laugh that felt less than humor-filled. "Do be extra kind to Miss Quinn and her family when they arrive, though."

A brief expression crossed Vernon's face, as though he was slightly offended that Edward would imply he'd be anything but welcoming to the Flynns and Mary, but the expression swiftly faded. "Yes, sir."

Edward made his way down the hall and to the parlor. The door was slightly ajar, so he could hear his family before he saw them. Masculine voices murmuring with the occasional lilt of female ones. So his brothers were here.

It wasn't until he reached the door that he could make out

the words.

"…not certain what to think of it. But then I feel I haven't truly known Edward since Alice's death, and that was three years ago."

Edward flinched. The voice belonged to his younger brother by two years, Evan.

"Edward allows close those who he wants close." The second voice was his youngest brother, Gabriel, who was four years his junior. "We have not been in that circle for a very long time."

Edward drew a sharp breath. His brothers had once been his best friends. And they were right that he had pushed them away after Alice's death. He had tried to protect them from the truth. Tried to protect himself from it.

He pushed the door open before he could overhear more censure and stepped inside. "Good afternoon," he said, his voice tight and hard.

His brothers were standing at the sideboard and both turned to watch him enter while his mother and sister rose from their place together on the settee.

For a moment, Edward only stared at them all. They looked so much alike, so much like *him*, and when they were all together, their presence tugged at his gut. He had once turned to them for solace, for support. Now they stared at him like he was a stranger in their midst.

"Darling," his mother said, moving toward him to kiss both his cheeks, one after the other. "I am so happy you've arrived."

He smiled down at her. "I'm pleased to be here."

Audrey sidled in as her mother stepped aside. His sister searched his face, her expression one of deep concern, and he turned away from it, not wanting her to find whatever she sought. When he did so, she sighed softly.

"Good afternoon, Edward," she said softly, disappointment lacing her tone.

His brothers now moved forward together. Evan offered

his hand first, hesitant. "Edward."

And if Evan was hesitant, Gabriel's hostility was only barely veiled as he shook Edward's hand in turn.

"I'm so glad you're all here," Edward said with a false smile. "I know Mary is very much looking forward to meeting the entire family."

Gabriel let out a grunt of displeasure and returned to the sideboard, where he splashed liquor into a tumbler. As he lifted it to his lips, he snapped, "But we aren't all here, are we?"

Their mother turned on him with a gasp. "Gabriel!"

Edward flinched. His brother was, of course, referring to his twin sister, Claire. Beautiful Claire who had run off to marry a charlatan and a bastard. She hadn't been heard from for over a year beyond cryptic letters she wrote only to Gabriel.

Claire who had sent a ripple through this family as deep and impactful as Alice, herself, had.

"Of course, I mean everyone but Claire," Edward said softly, watching his brother down his drink in an angry slug. "Have you—have you heard from her?"

Gabriel's lips pinched. "Not for over a month," he growled. "But why do you care? You don't even remember she exists!"

Edward sucked in his breath at his youngest brother's rage, but before he could say anything to defend himself, their mother stepped between them.

"Enough," she said firmly. "This is not the time to discuss Claire." Her voice trembled as it always did when she said her missing daughter's name. "We are here to celebrate Edward's upcoming wedding to Miss Quinn."

Gabriel's hands were still clenched at his sides, his face an angry mask, but Evan and Audrey did not seem to share his contempt, for both of them moved forward.

"Yes, although it is a surprise, I am happy for you, Edward," Audrey said.

"But what can you tell us?" Evan pressed. "I don't think I've even met this girl, though I think she may be related to the

Hartholm duchy, yes?"

Edward nodded. "Her sister is married to the brother of the Duke of Hartholm. Hartholm and the duchess helped her in Society for the last year and a half."

"And you just saw this girl and felt you had no choice but to…what? Woo her? After hiding away for three years like a hermit?" Gabriel asked, his tone more flat and emotionless than Evan's or Audrey's or his mother's.

Edward turned on his brother, longing for reconnection. A desire he feared he would never see fulfilled when Gabriel turned his face so he wouldn't have to look at Edward.

"I'm surprised Audrey didn't tell you," he said.

"She did. I would simply like to hear something from you for once," Gabriel muttered.

Edward clenched his hands at his sides. His reticence to share his life, his past, his feelings, had truly damaged his relationships with his family. Perhaps irreparably when it came to Gabriel. He regretted that deeply, but had no idea how to even begin to change his path. There was so much they didn't know. So much he couldn't find the strength to say.

"I did see Mary and was drawn to her," he admitted slowly, unaccustomed to sharing anymore. "Yesterday at the garden party I…I took things too far. We were caught in a somewhat compromising position by her father. Obviously that meant I had to do the right thing."

"Lord Perfection mops up a mess again," Gabriel said.

Evan stepped forward, shooting their brother a glare that was obviously meant to silence him. "But what do you think of this Mary Quinn? Audrey says that the young woman is nice enough, but to tie your life to her when you know so little?"

Edward let his mind drift for a bare moment. Drift to Mary and her soft smiles. Mary and her gentle spirit. Mary's touch. And he couldn't help but feel lighter as he said, "I know more than enough to know I should do this, Evan. And I hope that once you all meet her, you will approve of my choice and wish us well."

"I will wish you well no matter what," Evan said.

Edward drew back at the earnestness of his brother's expression. It seemed that if Gabriel wanted to sever their relationship entirely, Evan was just as driven to repair it. For the first time since Alice ripped his soul to shreds, Edward thought it might be possible.

"Is there anything else we should know about Miss Quinn before her arrival?" his mother asked, slipping to his side to take his arm.

Edward looked down at her. She had aged so much since his wedding to Alice. The loss of her daughter and the estrangement between him and the others had obviously taken its toll. He covered her hand at his arm with his own.

"That she is a very light and happy spirit," he said. "I know that her pedigree likely means little to you, but she has endured a great deal living with a father who is...well, Sir Oswald is not ideal in any way."

He frowned as he thought of the way his future father-in-law lorded over Mary and crowed in his attempts to ruin her in order to force their marriage. Flynn seemed to hate the man just as intensely as Edward was beginning to.

Perhaps together they could give him a bit of comeuppance.

His mother worried her lip but nodded. "I look forward to her arrival."

No sooner had the words been spoken when Vernon stepped into the open doorway and said, "Mr. and Mrs. Flynn and Miss Quinn."

Edward found himself releasing his mother gently, moving toward the door where Mary would soon enter, his heart racing in anticipation that had nothing to do with his family and everything to do with her. And when she stepped into the room behind Gemma and Flynn, he realized that despite the circumstances of their engagement, he was truly looking forward to the life they would share. He only hoped she felt some version of the same anticipation, for he didn't want another marriage to a person who didn't care for him as much as he did for her.

Mary could hardly breathe as she stepped into the parlor and looked around the room. Her eyes immediately found Edward and some of her anxiety faded. He looked so happy to see her, and her heart leapt. The last two years of her life had been spent with the Flynn family, nearly all of whom were married to people they loved. She had watched their connections with a twinge of jealousy and longing. She had prayed she would find something similar.

And now here was Edward, walking toward her. And she knew she could and *was* falling in love with him.

"Mary," he said, taking her hands in his despite the room being full of his family. He held her hands for a moment too long and then they both blushed as he looked at her brother-in-law and sister.

"Mr. and Mrs. Flynn, hello," he said.

Gemma arched a brow, her gaze darting between them. Gemma had been mostly quiet thus far about the engagement, but now Mary saw her sister's face begin to relax. As if she saw Mary's happy future as plainly as Mary was beginning to.

"Good afternoon, my lord," Gemma said.

"Woodley," Crispin said, his voice still gruff when he greeted her fiancé, but his handshake firm.

Knowing what she did about their past, she could see why Crispin would hesitate about her marriage, but she hoped he would accept it in time. That the men could truly be friends.

Edward slipped his hand into her arm and gently guided her away from her family and toward the large group of people waiting for her. She caught her breath a second time, for they did all look so much alike. And she could see their hesitation as they stared at her.

And given the circumstances, why wouldn't they be uncertain about her?

"Miss Mary Quinn, may I present to you my mother, the dowager Marchioness of Woodley," he said, moving her toward the older woman in the middle of the room.

Mary curtsied to the lady, hoping she was executing the move properly. She had done it what seemed like thousands of times in her life, but in this moment she felt awkward and foolish.

"Good afternoon, Miss Quinn," the dowager said as she stood.

Mary could see the lady sizing her up and wondered how much this important family knew about her grasping father, about her sister's two forced marriages. She flushed.

"G-good afternoon," she managed to stammer out.

Lady Woodley stepped forward and examined her closely. "You are a very pretty thing, that is plain. But tell me, young lady, what do you think of my son?"

Mary almost staggered at both the unexpected compliment and the direct question. She shot Edward a glance. He looked rather embarrassed, but did not intervene. In fact, he seemed to be waiting for her answer as much as everyone else in the room now was.

And what should she say? There were so many pretty, proper answers, but in the end, she decided to settle on the truth.

"I have found your son very interesting from the first moment I met him, my lady," she admitted on a hot blush. "And the more I have come to know him, the more I admire him. I realize the circumstance of our engagement may not recommend me to you, but I hope you will give me the chance to prove that I will make him as good and faithful a wife as I can."

Lady Woodley arched a brow at her words, and for a moment panic gripped Mary. Had she said too much? Gone too far?

But then the lady smiled and suddenly her stern face was far more open. In that moment, Mary saw that she was where Edward had gotten his beautiful dark eyes.

"I am so very happy to welcome you to our family," Lady Woodley said as she reached out to take Mary's hand. She squeezed it gently before she drew Mary forward. "I think you know my daughter Audrey a little."

Mary nodded. "Oh yes, we have been at many gatherings together."

Audrey smiled at her. "And every time I saw you I wanted so much to approach you, but one thing or another prevented it. I have an idea that we will be kindred spirits, Miss Quinn."

Mary couldn't help her widening smile. "I hope so, Lady Audrey.

"My brothers," Edward continued, guiding her to the two men standing at the sideboard. "The elder is Evan, the younger Gabriel."

Evan stepped forward first, hand extended. Mary could see the uncertainty in his eyes as he spoke to her, welcomed her as the rest had. But there was also kindness there, she thought, perhaps some kind of hope mixed with the trepidation. She knew their family was fractured. Perhaps she could help repair it. She owed it to Edward to try, at least.

"My lord," she said, moving her attention to Gabriel. He had a more sullen appearance than his two brothers and his frown was deeper.

"Miss Quinn," he drawled, and looked past her to Edward. "I'm sorry you will not get to meet my twin, Claire. But she is not with us at present. Is she, Edward?"

The flinch that rippled through Edward could be felt by anyone within a foot of him and Mary squeezed her eyes shut briefly. "I did not realize Lady Claire was your twin," she said, forcing herself to remain clam. "I'm sorry I do not get to meet her this time and I hope to someday have that pleasure."

Gabriel's gaze flitted to her at her calm and polite response and he nodded briefly. "As do I, Miss Quinn. More than you know."

Audrey rushed forward in an obvious attempt to ease some of the tension that had filled the room at the mention of the missing Woodley. "And the only other member of the family missing is Jude—Mr. Samson."

Mary blinked up at Edward. "Mr. Samson?"

"My man of affairs," he explained with an odd look for his sister. "He is presently in the country dealing with a personal matter. He should be back in time for the wedding."

"He is like another brother," Audrey continued, looking to the three men for confirmation. It was one they all readily gave with their nods.

"And this is Mary's sister, Gemma Flynn, and her husband Crispin Flynn," Edward added, motioning to Gemma and Crispin, who had been watching the familial interaction with what Mary recognized was deep interest. If her sister's smile as she stepped forward was any indication, she approved of this Woodley clan. Crispin was slower and his smile was less certain, but he too shook hands and made the kind of small talk expected at a first meeting of future relatives.

Mary sighed as Lady Woodley took over as hostess and offered seats and refreshment. Any minor qualms aside, this first meeting had gone better than she could have hoped. This was a family she could feel comfortable belonging to, just as she felt comfortable with her brother-in-law's family, the Flynns.

And while the Woodleys were perhaps not quite as notorious, she had a feeling they had a bit more depth than their title implied.

"Are you well?" Edward asked, his mouth suddenly close to her ear, his breath stirring her sensitive flesh and making her shiver uncontrollably.

"Yes," she gasped, tilting her face to look up at him. "I was just thinking how perhaps everything will be all right after all."

He smiled. "I think it will, Mary. For the first time in a

long time, I think it will."

CHAPTER SIX

Mary stood in front of the full-length mirror in her dressing room and swung her hips as she stared at her reflection. This was the third dress she had tried on, and she glanced at Gemma over her shoulder.

"Do you think the blue suits me?"

Gemma laughed. "You are beautiful, Mary. All colors suit you. Honestly, my dear, choose a gown or you shall be late for your own engagement ball."

Mary turned to face her sister, heat filling her cheeks. "I hope you don't think me vain," she said. "It is only that tonight is such an important night and I want to look my best. I know that there are those who are talking about my marriage to Edward. They are whispering about how I trapped him. They're talking about how beneath him I am. I only want to make him proud."

The teasing light left Gemma's eyes in an instant and she moved forward to take both Mary's hands. "Someone will always whisper," Gemma said softly. "Our father has made that far too easy. But in the end, what matters is what Edward thinks."

Mary nodded, allowing her thoughts to drift to the man, himself. In the two weeks since they had become engaged, he had quite easily begun to wend his way into her mind and her heart.

"Your smile is so dreamy," Gemma teased. "And even if it weren't, I have watched you and your fiancé as you two have spent time together. I see your connection growing."

A thrill shot through Mary at her sister's observation. She had felt the same, but to know it was obvious to others was a comfort. Each day she and Edward spent together—which had been every day since their unexpected engagement—was like a slowly opening gift. They had walked together in the park, stolen quiet moments at balls and parties and they had spoken of the future and the life they wanted to lead. He liked the same books she did, he enjoyed art and was already planning trips for them to museums all over London and even abroad once they were wed.

All her attraction based upon his handsome face was now strengthened by how fascinating she now found his soul, his spirit.

"You care for him," Gemma said softly.

Mary nodded without hesitation. "The more I come to know him, the closer we become, yes, I am beginning to care very deeply." She shifted and gave her sister a side glance. "He is very…he's quite…when he touched me, I…"

She trailed off with a furious blush burning her cheeks and chest. Gemma turned her face.

"I understand. What you are feeling is desire and it is perfectly natural to experience it. Woodley is a very handsome man."

Mary shivered. That was an understatement if any had ever been made. He was more than handsome. He was devastatingly beautiful. His image haunted her daydreams and her sleepless nights. It inspired very wicked thoughts and longings.

"Very," she said instead of voicing her inappropriate thoughts aloud. "I think I finally understand the looks you and Crispin exchange when you think I cannot see you."

Gemma's eyes went very wide and her cheeks went from pale to pink to flaming red in a matter of seconds. She smoothed her skirts with a laugh. "I—oh, goodness. Well, we will cover what will happen on your wedding night after this final reading of the banns this weekend."

"Can you believe it is only a week after that that I'll wed?" Mary asked.

Gemma slipped an arm around her and squeezed. "No. I cannot believe it."

The catch in her sister's voice made Mary turn toward her. Tears sparkled in Gemma's eyes and Mary gasped as she embraced her.

"Oh, please don't be upset," she burst out.

Gemma laughed as she embraced her. "It is not upset, I assure you, my love. It is only that I spent so many years terrified our father would destroy you. He might have done his best, but I think you are going to be happy. And that makes *me* so happy."

Tears welled in Mary's eyes to match her sister's. "I feel the same way about you. Seeing you so happy with Crispin and Esmeralda, it pleases me to know that despite all of Father's best efforts, he could not destroy us."

Gemma touched her cheek. "Not at all." She shook her head. "But here we are gabbing away, and downstairs Crispin and Edward are waiting for us. Come, let us call for your maid and fix your hair."

Mary smiled as she watched her sister walk away, but their conversation lingered in her mind. She had spent so much of her life waiting for something terrible to happen that now that those times were over, she almost didn't know what to do with herself.

She could only hope these happy times would last.

Edward watched as Flynn paced to the sideboard and held up a bottle of sherry. "Drink?"

He shook his head slightly. "None for me."

Flynn shrugged and set the bottle away untouched. Edward couldn't help but follow the action with his stare. "You do not drink anymore?"

The question was far too personal for their strained acquaintance, a fact proven by Flynn's sharp glance at him. But then the other man shrugged. "I find I do not need to drown myself anymore. Not since Gemma."

Edward cleared his throat. "It occurs to me that though we have danced around the subject, we have never directly discussed Alice. Not with each other, at any rate."

He thought he saw Flynn shoot a second quick look at the liquor, but he didn't touch it before he crossed the room to stand beside the mantel. He faced Edward, his expression impassive.

"I suppose we did not. At first because we were rivals for her so-called affection. Later because we were both victims of her. But you did me a kindness, Woodley, by exposing her true character. You helped save me from doing something stupid, something that would have made me lose Gemma. And so if you would like to discuss your late wife now, I will do so."

Edward squeezed his eyes shut. Two years ago, he had given over Alice's diary and her suicide note to Gemma Flynn. They had been a way to prove to Crispin that Alice was not the angel he had built up in his mind. Edward had never regretted doing it.

"I don't hate you," he offered. "Do you hate me?"

Flynn sighed. "Once I did. A very long time ago. But, you know, I always hated myself more. For not saving her. Now I know I couldn't have. She didn't *want* to be saved. She wanted to destroy."

"It was all she was capable of," Edward said softly.

Flynn nodded. "But Mary is capable of so much more. She is not like Alice, not in any slight way."

Edward jerked his head toward his future brother-in-law, surprised that he had shifted the conversation to Mary. But then, why wouldn't he? It was obvious Flynn cared deeply about his wife's sister.

"I can see that," Edward reassured him. "Her light from within is…it is uniquely her."

"She's been through a great deal," Flynn continued. "Her father's ways are…well, she saw Gemma suffer. She had to fear every day for her own welfare."

Edward squeezed his hands at his sides. "The idea that she had to live that way makes my blood boil."

A shadow of a smile crossed Flynn's face. "I have stood by silently in the face of his behavior, waiting for the moment when Mary was safe and I could turn my full wrath on that scheming bastard."

Edward lifted both brows. "You have plans for him?"

"Oh, yes."

"I would very much like to be a part of them," Edward said without hesitation.

Flynn stared at him, as if sizing him up for a moment. Then he nodded. "I think together we could ensure that bastard suffers nicely for what he did to our wives."

Edward wanted to elaborate. To scheme, but before they could, the door behind them opened and Gemma and Mary entered the parlor. All thoughts of vengeance or Alice or anything else unpleasant emptied from Edward's head, replaced by only the vision that was Mary.

She was utterly beautiful in a pale blue gown stitched with yellow flowers. Her dark hair was spun up in a complicated fashion, leaving tendrils to frame her slender, beautiful face. She had never been so beautiful, and the pounding thud of desire that accompanied every moment he spent with her had never been so loud and strong.

"Good evening, gentlemen," Gemma said with a knowing smirk in his direction before she slipped from her sister to stand beside her husband. "I think Lord Woodley approves, Mary."

Mary's cheeks darkened with the most fetching blush. One

that crept down her chest and disappeared into the wonderfully low neckline of her pretty gown.

"Gemma," Mary protested softly.

Edward stepped forward to take her hands. "I most definitely approve."

Gemma took Flynn's arm and all but dragged him toward the door. "Come, Crispin, let us make sure the carriage is ready."

In the past, Flynn might have refused that very obvious ploy to leave Mary and Edward alone for a moment. But this time he said nothing, only nodded toward Edward as the two left the room. Left Edward alone with the most delectable, fascinating woman he had ever encountered.

"You look beautiful," he murmured, drawing her closer now that they were alone. "I feel as though I could lose control just looking at you."

Her eyes widened slightly. "Like what happened in the garden?"

He smiled. "So much further than in the garden. At some point your sister will take you aside and explain to you how much further we could have gone...damn, *should* have gone that day. But Mary, I want to promise you now that the first time I claim you as my wife, it will be good for you. There will be pleasure. So much pleasure."

He nearly balked at the direct, passionate words that were spilling from his lips. He had never been an orator or a poet, finding words of desire easy to find. But with Mary, he could have written sonnets.

"I have no doubt that you will make me very pleased," she whispered. "And I can't wait."

Edward stifled a groan, but he couldn't stop himself from pulling her against him. He lowered his lips to hers and kissed her for the first time in what felt like an eternity. Her lips parted and he tasted her, drinking in her sweetness, fantasizing about kissing every inch of her body as he did her lips and mouth.

When he forced himself to pull away, she was breathing hard.

"It feels like forever since we did that," she panted. "We have been utterly surrounded since the engagement. Even when we are alone, we're not alone. Chaperones abound!"

"We did give them reason to be cautious, I suppose, but I may die if we have to wait another ten days before the wedding," he agreed.

There was a slightly wicked light that entered her eyes as she looked at him. "We could always sneak away tonight."

He lifted both brows. "From our engagement ball?"

She nodded. "Serafina and Rafe are hosting us and I have been to their home what seems like a hundred times. They have the sweetest little hidden room just behind the east entrance to the ballroom. I think it is a preparation room, but no one ever uses it. We could find our way there tonight."

Edward could actually feel the throb of his pulse in his rapidly hardening cock. Alone with Mary in a tiny room, no one around to disturb them. He could give her that first taste of pleasure right then and there. A secret only the two of them would know.

He swallowed. "Meet there at midnight, then?" he asked, his voice trembling.

"Come along, Mary, Edward!" Gemma called from the hallway. "The carriage is here."

Mary smiled as she leaned up to press a second, sweet kiss to his lips. "I'll be there if you will."

She turned and moved to join her sister and brother-in-law in the foyer and Edward watched her go. There was a stirring in his heart that he had not felt for a long time.

He was falling in love with this girl. And not like he had with Alice, in a burst of lightning inspired by her beauty and manipulations he had not seen until it was too late to go back. No, this was something different. Something special. Something *real*.

And someday soon, perhaps after they wed and their lives

calmed down, he would tell her those words. Better yet, he had a sneaking suspicion she might say them back. So when he exited the foyer, he had a spring in his step and a lightness to his heart that he hadn't felt in years.

Mary could hardly concentrate as she bounced up on the balls of her feet and looked to the large clock beside the entrance to the ballroom. It was nearly twelve, just moments until her assignation with Edward.

The ball had been wonderful, of course, filled with friends and family who only wished her well. And her father. Who also wished her well in his own way, she supposed.

Just as that thought filled her mind, she turned to find the man, himself, standing beside her. He was listing slightly, obviously drunk on the Duke of Hartholm's spirits.

"Hello again, Father," she said, some of her pleasure fading as she watched him try to right himself from his cockeyed position. "You look as though you are enjoying yourself."

He sniffed. "Hartholm is trying to corral me into a corner away from the more important folk, as usual."

Mary could hardly contain her smile. Crispin's brother, the very handsome Duke of Hartholm, and his wife were two of the most wonderful people she had ever met. They had helped her in her failed recent attempts at finding a mate without ever judging her or making her feel like a disappointment.

And Hartholm was *very* good at managing her father.

"I'm certain His Grace wouldn't corral you," she said with a dismissive wave of her hand.

He caught it with a scowl. "I had a talk with your new little family, Mary."

She froze. "With the Woodleys?"

"Yes, Lady Woodley seems to think very highly of you

despite how you caught her son in a trap."

Mary's jaw dropped open. "How I—that was all *your* doing!"

"Once you are married, you will continue to sponsor me, Mary. Gemma has all this time and you will have even more access to the better life. Perhaps I could even court your new mother-in-law."

Mary drew back in horror. "Lady Woodley?"

He smiled. "She would raise my lot considerably, wouldn't she?"

The clock behind her chimed and Mary jumped.

"I have someone to meet, Father," she said, her pleasure for the night rapidly bleeding out in the face of his smug satisfaction. "Good evening."

He let her turn for a moment before he drew her back. "Don't foul this up, Mary. If you do, I promise you'll be sorry."

She shook his hand away and rushed blindly through the ballroom, past the smiling faces of her friends, through the crowds preparing to dance and revel in her happiness. A happiness she couldn't feel as she found the little side room tucked away behind a screen near the east entrance of the ballroom and stepped inside.

CHAPTER SEVEN

Mary shut the door behind herself and leaned against it in the dark, trying to catch her breath, trying to shake off the stench of her father's greedy and appalling behavior.

The sound of flint interrupted her attempts, and she gasped as light brightened the room. Edward stood near a worn-out settee, holding a candle. He had a lopsided smile on his very handsome face and Mary turned away so he wouldn't see the tears glistening in her eyes, the dismay she couldn't hide when the light hit her.

But looking away didn't help. His smile vanished and he rushed toward her with a gasp. "What is it?"

He lifted the candle to examine her, and she swallowed hard and fought for control. "It's nothing," she lied. "Nothing at all, Edward."

He set the candle down on a table and caught her shoulders in both hands. "Tell me the truth. What has put such an expression on your face at a ball that is meant to celebrate you?"

She swallowed hard. If she did as he asked, he could think less of her. Others had done so after seeing her father's worst true nature. But Edward was right that honesty was the best policy. He would find out soon enough at any rate.

"Oh, it's that I bumped into my father and he was just awful," she admitted. "He finally talked to your family, which

I'm certain will lower their estimation of me. Worse, he—he—
"

"He?" Edward encouraged.

Mary sucked in a breath that didn't feel like it helped it all. "Oh God. He threatened to *court* your mother, a thought that is stomach-turning enough. He also expects to be taken care of by you, as he has been by Crispin all these years. You have been trapped into a very lopsided bargain, Edward. You will probably come to regret it if my father has his way."

She sucked in a breath to continue her tirade, but when Edward glided his hands down her bare arms and caught her hands, the touch silenced her. She stared up at him, blinking as she awaited his response.

"Sweet, sweet Mary, please don't upset yourself," he said softly. "I assure you, I have warned my family about your father and they will not judge you because of him. Except to marvel, as I do, how you and your sister escaped his clutches to become such beautiful, proper ladies."

She sighed. "Oh, how humiliating that you had to *warn* your family about him. You may think they don't judge me but—"

"They don't," he said, his tone firm, brooking no further argument. "As for him courting my mother, I would like to see him try. She would put him out on his ear!"

He laughed and Mary couldn't help but join in. "I-I don't know Lady Woodley as well as you do, of course, but it is hard to picture her allowing my father's awkward wooing."

"Your father will calm down once we are wed," he reassured her.

She shook her head. "But with his 'assistance', everyone must think I am trapping you. Using my wiles to—"

He leaned in, and suddenly his mouth on hers, silencing her in the most pleasant way. She leaned up into him, wrapping her arms around his neck with a shuddering sigh as she allowed him to sweep her away.

"If anyone ever asks," he whispered as he swept his arm

beneath her knees and carried her to the settee behind them. "I will tell them I used my wiles on *you*. That I forced you to be my bride."

"So you intend to seduce me into marrying you?" she whispered, settling on the settee and staring up as he loomed over her.

"As often as I can," he said.

His mouth returned to hers, but this time there was more force to his kiss, more purpose. To her surprise, her entire body reacted in ways she had never experienced. All the tension from her encounter with her father bled away, replaced by tingling pleasure that started at her very private core and spread from there. Her skin was on fire, her nipples hardened, her legs clenched. It was like madness in physical form.

Only a madness she very much wanted to surrender to.

"Edward," she murmured as he broke from her lips and began to gently kiss her neck.

He looked into her eyes and she saw her own need reflected there. Harder, more certain, more experienced, but the same in its power and heat.

"I want to give you pleasure, Mary," he whispered.

She didn't really understand when he said those things. She felt so many things whenever he touched her, but this pleasure he spoke of was obviously different.

"H-how?" she asked.

He smiled, but there was hesitation in his eyes now. "By touching you. Intimately."

Her lips parted. She burned between her legs and the idea of him touching her there, easing that ache, was intoxicating and terrifying all at once.

"We're wed in just a bit over a week," he reassured her. "And I wouldn't claim you fully. As much as I want to, until you are mine I wouldn't. But won't you let me give you pleasure, Mary? Won't you let me make you moan my name?"

She swallowed hard. His voice was so seductive, his words even more so. And she had never wanted anything more than what he now offered, even if she didn't truly understand his words, his implications.

"I trust you," she murmured, reaching up to cup his cheek. He leaned into it, his eyes lighting up with such powerful emotion that she sucked in her breath.

"I will never give you a need to not trust me," he promised. Then his mouth was on hers again and she couldn't verbally respond. She simply returned his kiss, pouring all her growing feelings into the act.

His hand slid down her body, over her shoulder, until he cupped one breast and she arched despite the strange invasion. No one had ever touched her like that. It was wild and wicked and oh, so very naughty. And she liked it. Liked it even more when he began to stroke his thumb back and forth over the thin fabric, causing friction against her already hard and tingling nipple.

She caught her breath as the sensation crested over her in waves, making her weightless and hot as he continued to stroke her.

"So this is what you meant by pleasure," she gasped.

He chuckled, a very possessive and male sound. "Oh, no. Not even close yet."

He continued to stroke her nipple while with his opposite hand he glided down her stomach, her hip, her thigh. He began to bunch her gown up, tugging the fabric up to display her legs.

She blushed as he looked down to observe his handiwork. She had never been bared to a man before, and even though it was Edward and this was his right...or soon would be...she still felt exposed and uncertain.

He smiled at her to reassure her. "You are beautiful," he whispered. Her dress was now bunched at her waist and he rested his hand on her thigh. "You are certain?"

Her heartbeat was so loud in her own ears that she hardly understood his question. Certain? She was utterly uncertain of everything. Except him. Her faith in him was unshaken.

"Yes," she breathed.

He let out a low curse, his tone laced with relief. Then he slid his hand up, found the slit in her drawers, and his fingers slipped inside. He brushed the outer lips of her sex and she tensed at the gentle touch.

"You are already wet," he groaned.

She stared at him. Yes, she felt wet. Very wet. "Is that…is that a good thing?"

He nodded. "Very, very good," he promised. "It will make it easier when I—"

He broke off as he parted her lips and slipped a finger across her entrance.

"Oh!" she gasped as electric awareness sparked through her. It was strange but not unpleasant to be touched like this.

He smiled and kept moving his fingers over her. It was a slow rhythm he built as he moved over her, smoothing the wetness he had described over her. She began to arch against him out of pure instinct, reaching for something she didn't understand but now needed as much as she required breath or water or food.

"That's right," he encouraged her as his fingers pressed harder. One digit slipped inside of her and she gasped at the breach.

"Edward!" He wiggled the finger gently and she arched harder against him. "What are you doing to me?"

"Making you come," he explained, then pressed his thumb to a hidden bundle of exquisitely sensitive nerves at the top of her sex. When he touched her there, she jolted. Pleasure so intense it bordered on pain throbbed at the point of contact and she moaned.

"Not too loudly now," he said with a chuckle. "Or else they'll come to look for us."

She bit her lip as he increased his tempo, pumping his finger inside of her, stroking outside in time. She lifted, reached, searched, and finally the moment she had been seeking crashed over her. Pleasure came in waves, powerful crests that stopped her breath and doubled the rate of her heart.

He continued to stroke her through the explosion, watching her as she thrashed on the old settee.

Finally, she went limp, her body twitching a few last times. He smiled as he withdrew his hand from her, licked his fingers clean and then smoothed her dress down.

"I don't know if that makes it easier to wait or harder," he laughed, almost more to himself than to her.

She struggled to sit up. "Is that what will happen on our wedding night?"

He nodded. "Something like it. But instead of my finger inside of you, it will be this."

He took her hand and rested it between his legs. She felt the hard ridge of him beneath his trousers and her body shuddered without her meaning for it to.

"It's bigger," she whispered.

"Indeed," he said. "But you will be ready, just as you were today. And it will join us in a way that can never be changed or taken from us. You'll be mine then, in every sense of the word."

"And will you be mine?" she asked.

He stared at her for a long moment. "I'll be yours. Forever."

She leaned forward and rested her ear against his chest. She could hear the throbbing of his heart, faster than it should be because of what they had just done. She smiled at the sound, smiled at his promises.

"I can't wait," she whispered.

He nodded above her, his arms coming around her shoulders. "Neither can I. But we should go back to the ball. I'm certain you will be missed."

She lifted her head with a sigh and looked up at him. "Back to reality again, then."

He smiled. "But soon *this* will be our reality, Mary. And then the waiting will be worth it."

He got to his feet and helped her to hers, smoothing her dress and tucking an errant curl behind her ear. She leaned up and pressed her lips to his as he did it, and she felt his heat and his hunger when he returned her kiss.

When he pulled away, his hands were shaking. "Back you go," he urged her as he tugged the door open and made certain no one was watching as she slipped out into the buzz of the ballroom.

She smiled at him over her shoulder before she moved to the other side of the screen and back to the party outside. But as he left her sight, her smile only grew wider. Soon the man behind her would be her husband. And for the first time in a very long time, the future was a moment she looked forward to rather than feared.

CHAPTER EIGHT

Mary was still buzzing with pleasure the next day as she took her tea alone in the parlor. Gemma had not been well that morning and so she had left Mary to rest as she took a nap.

"I wonder if she'll have another baby," Mary mused out loud.

The words made her smile, not just for her sister and Crispin, but for herself. After all, in another week she would be wed and her own baby could be made any time after that. Her baby with Edward. A fine and happy thought, indeed. One she laughed about as the door opened and Crispin's butler entered the room.

"You have a note, miss," he said as he held out a tray with a folded sheet of paper perched on it.

"Thank you, Fletcher," she said as she took it.

"Would you like anything, miss?" he asked.

She stared at her name, written in a hand she didn't know, and shook her head in distraction. "No, thank you. I'm fine."

He bowed slightly and left her alone. She broke the seal on the paper and opened it. The same elegant hand that had written her name had written the following ugly words: *If you do not want your fiancé destroyed, you will meet with us today. Alone. At two.*

An address followed, on one of the most fashionable streets in London. Mary caught her breath. Was this a joke?

The names signed below the short note seemed familiar. *Isadora and Imogen Brookfield.*

Brookfield...why was that name so recognizable? She squeezed her eyes shut and conjured an image of two icy blonde women. Unpleasant yet always invited to activities hosted by the *ton*. Mary had only ever met the two once or twice, at balls. As far as she could recall, they had never had any real interaction.

So why would they write to her and threaten Edward?

Her breath caught. When she had been told about Alice, she had done a little research on the woman who had been Edward's first wife. Hadn't her name been Brookfield before she became marchioness?

Were these two women related to the one who had all but destroyed Edward with her schemes?

"If they are, they might truly have a way to hurt him," Mary murmured.

She looked toward the door. She could take this note to Gemma. Her sister would advise her, she might even know more about the pair, considering Crispin's involvement with Alice all those years ago.

But Gemma would also certainly forbid her to meet with them. Or insist upon accompanying Mary to see them, which might rile the women and cause Edward even more pain.

Mary paced the room. If she went alone, as was the request, she would not be in physical danger, certainly. She couldn't picture those perfectly manicured women harming her and causing a scandal. She could find out their intentions and then go to her sister and her fiancé with all the available information.

"Yes," she whispered to herself, the word making her heart rate increase exponentially. She moved to the door and rang. When Fletcher reappeared, she said, "In about an hour I'll need the carriage to make a call."

He nodded. "Certainly, miss."

"And will you send my maid to my chamber to help me

prepare?"

"Of course." He gave her an odd look and Mary briefly wondered if the color was well and truly gone from her cheeks. She certainly felt drawn out by this strange request and the threat that accompanied it.

But until she met with the Brookfields, there was no way to guess what awaited her. She could only try to control her fear as she readied herself for an encounter that was bound to be anything but pleasant.

The Brookfield house was very large, very intimidating and very cold. As the butler stepped aside to let her in, Mary actually lifted her hands to cover her arms in the hopes of rubbing the gooseflesh away.

"Your maid may accompany me belowstairs," the servant intoned as he looked Mary up and down with a sniff. "In the meantime, *you* will come with me."

He shot her maid a look that seemed to freeze the girl in place and then began to take long strides down the hallway. Mary struggled to keep up and followed him into a parlor that was just as unwelcoming as the rest of the house.

The servant said nothing else, nor did he offer her refreshment as he pulled the door shut behind him and left Mary alone to await her...what would she call the two? Summoners?

She paced the room, staring at the beautiful yet utterly uncomfortable furniture, the emotionless family portraits. One caught her eye and she moved closer. The placard read *Alice*.

She drew back in surprise as her eyes darted up to examine the face. Mary worried her lip. Alice had been truly beautiful, with blonde hair and pale blue eyes. She had a slender face, an elegant, long neck and high cheekbones. She was classically beautiful, and yet there was a cruelty to her face. A mocking turn to her lips. Did Mary see it there because of what she already knew?

Or was it just that the portrait maker had seen fit to reflect her true self in his painting?

The door behind her clicked and she turned to find two women standing in the room. Twin images of each other and an echo of the woman in the portrait behind her, they smirked first at her and then at each other.

"Comparing yourself to our dear sister?" one of them said as she stepped forward.

"She falls short, doesn't she?" the other cackled.

Mary swallowed hard. "It is Imogen and Isadora, yes?"

One of them shrugged. "I'm Imogen."

Mary nodded, making a note that Imogen was wearing a red sash to her sister's blue as a way to tell them apart. "Good afternoon to you both. I was surprised to receive your missive."

Imogen laughed, an ugly, dry sound that lacked pleasure of any kind. "I assume you already knew about our sister's existence."

Mary nodded as she glanced at the portrait from the corner of her eye. "So she *was* your sister. The resemblance is uncanny."

It was Isadora who responded, her hands fisted at her sides. "She was our beloved older sister, Miss Quinn. Who was ripped away from us thanks to that bastard you intend to marry."

Mary pinched her lips together. She hadn't been certain what to expect when she came here. This full-on attack had been on the list, but it still shocked her.

She tried to remain calm in the face of their bubbling rage. "I can only imagine what it must be like to lose your sister, especially in such a tragic manner. I too have an elder sister."

Imogen shook her head. "Gemma Flynn. Yes, we've had our dealings with her. She kicked us out of a ball once."

Mary drew back in surprise. Gemma, kick someone out of a ball? She could hardly imagine it. But then, Gemma was so protective of Crispin. A feeling Mary was beginning to mirror when it came to Edward.

"Have we ever paid back Mrs. Flynn for that, sister?" Isadora asked.

The two women exchanged a glance, and Imogen smiled. "I think *this* will suffice, sister."

Mary fisted her hands at her sides. Edward had described Alice's potential for cruelty, wrapped up in a beautiful mask. She thought she was seeing a glimpse of what he had endured, through the actions and bitter words of her sisters. This was a family of monsters, created by what horrors, she could not imagine.

But they made her father look almost tame in comparison.

"Enough," she said softly. "You have made a threat against my future husband and it is clear by your attitudes now that you mean it. You asked me here, so tell me what you think you can do to him and what you want from me in order to protect him."

"Sit," Isadora said, pointing to the settee that faced Alice's bitter little portrait.

Mary folded her arms. "I prefer standing where I am, thank you."

The twins flounced to the settee and sat together, watching up at her with hatred burning in their eyes. But there was also pain. Despite their cruelty, she could see they did love the sister whose painted glare she felt behind her. They loved Alice and they blamed Edward for her fall.

"Do you know what your fiancé did to our sister?" Isadora asked. "Did he tell you anything about her?"

Mary hesitated. "He said that she was unhappy and she threw herself down the stairs, killing herself and their unborn child."

Isadora shook her head. "That wasn't what he told you. I would wager he said she was wicked. But she only wanted what she wanted. If he was not capable of giving it to her, that was *his* failing. He drove her to hurt herself, to prove to him how serious she was. And it is his fault she is dead, buried in the cemetery only because we paid off the vicar not to label her as a suicide."

Again, Mary felt the pain radiating from these women and she felt for them despite their vows to hurt Edward. Perhaps they could be reasoned with.

"I cannot imagine your loss," she said, taking the seat across from them at last. "I am very sorry. But you have threatened Edward and you cannot think that harming him in some way will change things."

Imogen's expression tightened, anger like a mask on her face. "He does not suffer like we do. He was glad to be rid of her—you could see the relief on his face the moment she was declared dead. He destroyed her and now he will move on? Marry? Have children? Be happy? While she rots?"

Mary held her tongue, because she could not deny this woman's words. The sisters did not see Alice in a negative light. They either accepted Alice for what she was or simply refused to see her bad behavior as a problem. How could they do anything but hate Edward? Hate Crispin? Hate everyone they strove to blame for Alice's disturbing actions?

"He *must* suffer," Isadora added, her voice like the hiss of a snake. "You will not marry him, Miss Quinn."

Mary bolted from the chair and stared down at them. They had serene expressions on their faces at last, as if this pleased them in some way.

"I beg your pardon, but I certainly will," she said, trying to keep her tone calm.

"No," Isadora said. The two women rose together. "You will not."

"And why wouldn't I?" Mary whispered, fearful of the answer.

"Because if you insist upon marrying him next week, *we* will insist upon going to the magister," Isadora continued. "You see, my sister and I have strong beliefs that Alice did not throw herself down those stairs that day. We think Lord

Woodley may have pushed her."

As Mary's lips parted in understanding, Imogen continued, her smile wide and her voice suddenly dripping with innocence. "Yes. We kept it to ourselves out of respect to our poor, dead sister. And there is the fact that horrible Woodley *threatened* us. But now that you are engaged to him, we cannot stay silent. You see, now we fear for *your* life, my dear."

Mary stepped backward. "That is not true and you know it. There was a suicide note. There was a journal Edward told me you both saw. You *know* Alice's intent, you know perfectly well that everything that happened was designed to hurt Edward. She arranged for her 'fall', her 'suicide attempt' out of selfish manipulation."

"A journal? A note? No one but Edward and the two of us ever saw those things, not even the rest of our family. To protect our sister's reputation, our understanding is that Edward destroyed them." Imogen's smile broadened. "We will claim we never saw a note, but that her journal spoke of her fear of Edward and her desire to protect her child."

"No one will believe you," Mary said. "Edward is a respected marquis."

Isadora shrugged. "Perhaps it will go nowhere legally, although I'm certain there will be a long and drawn out investigation that will drag that whole Woodley family through the mud where they belong. He might be convicted of the crime. He might not. Either way, he will be destroyed."

"How?" Mary asked the question, although she could see the answer dancing in the eyes of the twins.

"There have been faint whispers regarding Alice's death for years," Imogen said.

"Whispers encouraged by you," Mary growled.

Imogen smiled, all but verifying the accusation. "If our story becomes public, there will be many who believe his guilt. He will be shunned, and if he is shunned by the right few, then *all* will follow. His sister and his brothers and his nasty mother will all be destroyed. His happiness and the future of any children he sires will be tarnished."

Mary's hands shook. She tried to stop the motion, tried not to let them see her weakness, but it was impossible. Her emotions were now too high. Her anger and her heartbreak out of control.

"Your sister died years ago," she whispered, hating that her voice trembled. "Why not just do this to him then?"

"Because Edward was punishing himself perfectly well on his own," Imogen said. "Hiding away like a hermit, cutting himself off from his family. He didn't even stop his sister from getting herself married off to a rogue who only wanted her for her money."

Isadora laughed. "That was my favorite part."

Mary moved toward them. "You are monsters."

The two women exchanged a glance, then dissolved into peals of laughter that grated against Mary's ears. She flinched away, though she didn't dare put her back to them.

"We were happy to let him rot, keeping our ability to turn the world against him in our pocket until the right time," Imogen said. "And this is the *perfect* time."

"Why?" Mary's mouth felt very dry as she forced the word from her lips.

Imogen frowned. "My sister and I slipped into your little engagement party last night, you know. We saw you together, so happy. He loves you, I think."

"Disgusting pig," Isadora interrupted, venom dripping from her words.

"Yes, dear. A disgusting pig who will suffer all the more when Miss Quinn here breaks off their engagement and tells him she does not want him. Back to his hovel he will go, drowning in loss. The *ton* will chatter about the reason and he may never come out again."

Mary blinked, digesting their words, their threats. Trying to find a way to battle them. But the women were right. If they went public with an accusation that Edward had murdered his pregnant wife, there were some in Society who would latch on to that juicy rumor like a dog with a thick bone. Even if he was declared innocent, the scandal would last far longer in the memories of those who loved to follow such things.

"Edward truly loved your sister," she began, desperate to save him. Save them. "He told me so himself. When she betrayed him with my brother-in-law, when she hurt herself in order to punish him, I promise you that it broke him. No marriage to me, no future happiness we might share, will ever completely heal that scar she left. He suffers—you needn't make him suffer more."

"Until he is dead in the ground, there will never be enough suffering," Imogen said, her tone utterly cold and strangely emotionless now.

Mary swallowed back the bile that rose in her throat. "Even if I walk away from Edward as you desire, how do I know you won't simply wait until a future time to hurt him? To do exactly what you describe next week or next year or in another three years?"

Isadora exchanged an almost blank look with her sister, as if they didn't understand the question. "You won't," she said. "But you'll know you saved him today, won't you? And maybe if he's miserable enough, we'll keep our accusations to ourselves. You'll only know for certain that we won't go after him now."

"That is hardly a bargain," Mary whispered, unable to speak in full voice as the weight of this conversation and the hatred of these women pushed down on her.

"You have one choice, my dear. End this engagement now. Today. If we do not hear from you that it has happened by two o'clock tomorrow afternoon, we are prepared to move forward with our plan. Is that clear?" Imogen asked.

"But—" Mary began.

"Is it clear?" Isadora barked.

Mary could hardly breathe. They had her cornered. There was no amount of reason or pleading that would change their minds. That fact *was* clear as the summer's day outside.

"I understand your meaning perfectly," she said, moving toward the door with as much dignity as she could muster when all she wanted to do was collapse in utter anguish.

"We look forward to you telling us you have done the right thing," Isadora called behind her, her voice now sickly sweet as pie.

Mary ignored her and entered the foyer. She found the door already open, the butler glaring at her as he motioned to the carriage that awaited her outside. Her maid was situated within, watching her through the open door with worry and confusion.

Mary said nothing as she entered the vehicle, nothing as the door was shut and they began to drive back toward Crispin and Gemma's home. She said nothing even as her maid questioned her.

There was nothing to say. Nothing to do. Only a decision to be made that had no happy ending.

CHAPTER NINE

"Are you well?" Gemma asked.

Mary jolted from her thoughts and looked down the table toward her sister and Crispin. She found them both staring at her, expressions of kind concern mirrored on both their faces.

"You are so quiet," Crispin added. "And you've hardly eaten."

Mary stared down at her plate, left untouched for so long that the food no longer even looked appetizing. "I—" she began, but then stopped herself.

She *could* tell Crispin and Gemma what had happened. But how could they help? The choices she had to make would remain the same. And knowing Crispin, he would try to rush in to save the day, and that might only drive Isadora and Imogen to hurt Edward even more. Perhaps the sisters might even decide to include Crispin and Gemma in their destructive plans. After all they had made it clear the Flynns were nearly as hated by them as Edward was.

"You...?" Gemma encouraged when Mary didn't finish her thought.

Mary blinked. "I am not feeling well, I fear," she lied. "Perhaps whatever little ailment you suffered this morning is catching, Gemma."

Her sister blushed, and Mary thought she heard Crispin mutter, "I hope not, at least not until after you are married."

She frowned. So she had guessed correctly. Gemma was with child again. Another reason not to drag her and her husband into her troubles. This was a happy time for them, and they deserved that.

"I think I will excuse myself and lie down a while, if you don't mind," she said, rising to her feet with a weak smile.

Crispin stood as well, and Gemma said, "Of course. Perhaps a good night's sleep will make you feel better."

Mary nodded, bid her goodnights and slipped from the room. She stumbled as she made her way up the stairs, tears welling up in her eyes. She had struggled with her decision for hours, trying to find a way to protect Edward, but also still be with him.

But there was none. Every choice she considered meant pain for someone. Every choice made one fact abundantly clear.

She loved this man. She wasn't *falling* in love with him, she didn't *think* she could love him at some future date—she loved him. Here and now. With all her heart. And that made the situation so much worse. Because she loved him, she wanted to be with him more than anything, because she loved him, she had to let him go.

And hope that the damage caused by the broken engagement would be enough for Isadora and Imogen.

She moved into her chamber on heavy feet and shut the door behind her, leaning against the barrier with a heavy, sobbing sigh.

"Is this truly what I am about to do?" she asked, flinching away from the words as they pierced the silence.

There was no answer from her silent room. Only the one in her heart. The one that could not save her from this path she had been thrust upon.

She was numb as she trod to the little escritoire that sat in the corner of her room. She could hardly see through her blurry vision as she drew out her pens and ink and a thick piece of paper. And she struggled for the words as she wrote and rewrote and rewrote a lie that would push Edward far away from her.

That would end her long-dreamed-of future and break her heart permanently.

Edward sat in his parlor, shifting uncomfortably on the settee as he forced a smile at his companions, his brothers Evan and Gabriel. What had possessed him to invite them to his home that night, he didn't know. At the time, he had hoped that perhaps there could be some reconciliation between them after his long hermitage.

But Evan only watched him and Gabriel sipped his drink sullenly.

"I cannot believe this wedding is a week from Sunday," Edward said.

Evan arched a brow. "I imagine that is true. After all, you hid from everything and everyone for so long. Then you burst back onto the scene and have a new bride within what, a month?"

"He's always moved swiftly when someone mattered to him." Gabriel said the words, but there was no kindness to them. "That is why our family concerns take so long."

Edward pushed to his feet and set his drink aside. "Is there something you wish to say to me, Gabriel?"

His youngest brother was on his own feet in an instant and rushed toward him. Edward realized Gabriel was going to hit him just a split second before Evan hurtled himself between them, shoving the men apart.

"Stop, Gabriel," Evan growled, holding their younger but very strong brother back with both hands.

"You let Claire run away, you didn't even look for her," Gabriel burst out, his own hands lowering from the fighting stance and going limp at his sides. "I know your wife died—

I'm certain her accident must have been terrible for you. But why couldn't you care about Claire instead of just yourself?"

Edward flinched. His brother was only saying the same words that sometimes echoed in his own head at night when he was alone in the dark. He stared at his two brothers now, thinking of how close they had once been. Until he chose to protect them from the truth...protect himself from having to say it out loud to people he loved.

"Alice didn't have an accident," he admitted. "She threw herself down the stairs. Worse yet, she was pregnant. We hadn't yet told anyone, but she killed the baby, too."

Both his brothers froze and Evan's arms dropped from Gabriel's chest in disbelief. "What?"

Edward swallowed. "Alice killed herself. In order to punish me for not being good enough. We told no one so that she would not be labeled a suicide."

"No one," Gabriel said, his eyes filled with pain, but this time some of it was for Edward rather than against him. "Not even your family."

"You don't know what she was like." Edward sat down hard back in his place. He cleared his throat and softly told them the truth about her. About them. About that horrible night that he had hidden from almost everyone he cared about. Before Mary, he had only ever told everything to his man of affairs, Jude Samson. When Gemma Flynn came to him, he'd told her a little, enough to help her, but not everything.

But now he faced his brothers. They both sat down as he spoke, their faces twisting with horror and finally understanding.

"Oh God, Edward," Evan whispered, his voice cracking. "That is a nightmare."

Edward looked at Gabriel. "I *know* I let Claire down, Gabriel. I let you down. But I could hardly move, hardly think, hardly function. By the time it registered what was happening, Claire was gone. I did send Samson to look for her. I *still* have men looking for her. But that does not excuse my lack of protection. And I am sorry every damned day, if that helps."

Gabriel seemed to struggle for an answer, his handsome face twisting as he fought between what was obvious empathy for Edward and desperate fear for their lost sister. But before he could respond, there was a light knock on the door and Edward's butler, Morris, stepped into the room.

"I'm sorry to disturb, my lords, but you have received a missive, Lord Woodley."

Edward managed to get to his feet and staggered to the door to take the message. He gave a half-hearted smile to his servant, then stepped back to his brothers as he looked at the note.

"It is from Mary," he said as he tugged the paper open. A truer smile passed his lips. Her sweetness was just what he needed to wash away the bitterness of his family's estrangement and his tale of Alice. Only as he read, the happiness he felt faded and he nearly dropped the message.

Evan got to his feet. "What is it? Is something wrong?"

Edward read the note a second time and then held it out to Evan. As his brother took it, he paced away to stand at the window, disbelief rocking him, holding him in his place as if he had been cast in stone.

"*Dear Lord Woodley,*" Evan began to read. He glanced up. "It is a bit formal of a start."

"You'll see why in a moment," Edward croaked as he waved his hand for his brother to continue.

Which he did. "As we have grown to know each other, there are aspects to your person that I feel will not match well with me. To prevent our mutual unhappiness, I have no choice but to end our engagement, effective immediately. Please do not come see me, as I do not believe we have anything left to discuss. Mary Quinn."

Gabriel had stood during the reading of Mary's note and he moved forward to snatch it from Evan and silently read over it a second time.

"That makes no sense," he said, shaking his head as he

looked at Edward.

Edward couldn't help but let his mind shift to another note he had found, this one from Alice. A note that laid out her hatred of him, her desire to hurt him by causing the death of their unborn child. He had been devastated by that night.

And yet Mary's words cut almost as deep in this charged moment.

"*Why* would she say this?" Evan asked. "I admit, I only know the young woman a little, but I have watched you two together. And as recently as last night, Gabriel and I were discussing how happy you looked, how well-matched despite the circumstances of your engagement."

Edward scrubbed a hand over his face, trying to think. It was so damned hard when everything hurt so much. It felt like he was on fire, staring with his heart, spreading to his entire person.

"We were happy," he choked out, thinking of Mary's sweet surrender in the little room near the ballroom at the Hartholm's ball not twenty-four hours ago. He wrinkled his brow. "We *are* happy."

Gabriel still held the note and read it a second time. "Could she have uncovered the truth about Alice somehow and it shocked her?"

He shook his head. "She knew the truth. I *had* to tell her because her brother-in-law, Crispin Flynn, shares a portion of the story." When his brothers stared at him in confusion, he waved them off. "It's a very long story and I swear to you I will tell you the whole sordid tale at some point. Right now I must focus on far more important things."

He halted as he said the words. *Far more important things.* Up until recently, his tangled, bitter past with Alice had been the most important thing. It had colored his every move, his every thought. His first wife's betrayal and her cruelty had defined him.

But now…now that was different. Because of Mary.

"I'm in love with her," he said softly, testing out the

words. They sounded like truth.

Evan moved toward him. "I see."

Gabriel set the note down on the table and leaned over it. "Her hand is shaky," he observed. "I saw her write something down for Mother a few days ago and it wasn't so shaky as this."

Edward stepped closer. His youngest brother had always had a head for details. "What else do you observe?"

Gabriel lifted the paper to the light. "Hmmm, there is a droplet of water here that dried. It could be a tear. She was obviously deeply upset when she wrote this."

Edward frowned. "I suppose that could be because she felt guilty for breaking off the engagement. Or fearful of what her father would do next."

"That is the oddest part, isn't it?" Evan interjected as he leaned over the letter with his two brothers. "We've all met her father and he's a lout. There is a sense of cruelty about him that I think proves true all her fears when it comes to her future if she's returned to his care. If she knew about Alice already, had told you that it was not something that troubled her, why would she choose her father's choices over her own? A man who could very well match her with someone far more terrible than you."

Edward shook his head. "She *wouldn't*."

Gabriel straightened up and met his stare. "You are sure."

"Absolutely. She's terrified of her father's influence, of being marched back into his home and used for whatever purpose he would desire. I cannot picture anything that would make her believe that was a better option than carrying on with our wedding."

Gabriel frowned. "Then we must consider that Mary might have been coerced into writing this letter."

Edward's heart shot into his throat. "I'm going to her."

Evan nodded. "You absolutely should do that. Great God, man, from what you described, you have already been through hell. And since you love this girl, I hope you'll be willing to fight for her."

Edward grabbed the letter from the table and shoved it into his pocket. "I'm willing to die for her," he declared, before waving to his brothers and darting out the door to call for his horse.

For years he had accepted whatever version of fate life had laid out before him, too exhausted by his experiences to fight for something different or better. But now everything had changed. The past few weeks with Mary had shown him a path that was filled with light and joy.

And he wasn't going to lose that—or her—without a fight worthy of David facing Goliath.

CHAPTER TEN

Mary lay in her bed, staring up at the canopy, but sleep would not come. She feared it might never come again, and that if it did, she would only be haunted by reminders of the living nightmare she currently inhabited.

Every word she had exchanged with Isadora and Imogen, every sentence she had written to Edward in her letter…they rang in her head, taunting her.

She slid the pillow from under her head and flopped it over her face, wishing that she could block out her thoughts as easily as she was able to block out the moonlight coming through the window or the sound of the crackling fire. She lay like that for a long few moments. Stifling in the quiet dark and yet her mind continued to race regardless.

"What did I do?" she wailed into the pillow at last. "What did I do?"

"You broke things off with me—quite foolishly, I might add."

Mary jolted at the sound of a voice in her room and threw the pillow away. She lurched to a seated position and her eyes flew to the window. Sitting on the ledge, arms folded and eyes locked on her, was Edward.

His expression was one of anger, one of confusion, but she also saw a hint of desire there and looked down to realize she was in her nightshift, which had a very low neckline. She lifted her hands to cover herself.

"Edward!" she cried. "What are you doing here? *How* did you get here?"

He pressed his lips together. "I climbed up that tree." He motioned behind him with a thumb. "And found your window happily unlatched. As for what I'm doing here, is that really a question you need to ask, my clever girl? My clever and oh-so-beautiful girl."

Everything in her wanted to close her eyes and savor the sound of his rough voice complimenting her. To rise up and go to him and make the last twelve hours go away.

Instead, she pulled the sheet up to cover herself more fully and clenched her jaw. She had to remain strong.

"Edward, I asked you not to come in my note. I do not—" She broke off as he pushed away from his seat at her windowsill and slowly came around the bed. He perched himself on the edge, too close. So close. "I-I do not want to see you."

He smiled at her stammering. "Don't you? Is that why your eyes dilate with desire? Why you keep looking at my lips?"

She folded her arms. "If my eyes dilate, it is to adjust to the low light in the room."

He tilted his head. "Don't be foolish, Mary."

"I'm not being foolish. I have said what I want to say and now I'm asking you to leave." She hoped her voice sounded stronger to him than it did to her.

"No." He said the one word slowly and succinctly, and she stared.

"No?"

"No," he repeated.

She scooted to the other side of the bed and put her feet on the floor. God, her nightgown felt revealing now. Especially with the moonlight behind her.

"If you won't leave because I asked, then I will call for the servants and they will put you out." She edged around the bed to her door as she said the words, watching him with every step.

He lifted both eyebrows. "I don't think you will."

She gasped. "How utterly ungentlemanly of you, Woodley! I have said I will do this, don't pretend as though I am a liar."

He stood up and took a long step toward her. "You are a liar."

Her lips parted, but still she didn't reach for the bell pull. It was like she couldn't.

"I am not," she whispered.

"You are, because you said you don't want me and I can see from your face and your trembling body that you do." He reached out and caught a lock of her hair that bounced around her shoulders. He coiled it around his fingers. "You are a liar and I came here to find out why."

She could hardly think when he was so close. She could smell his skin, for God's sake, and it was like heaven. But she couldn't let her physical needs, nor her deep feelings, keep her from her course. All this was to protect him, even if he didn't understand that.

"I told you in the letter," she said as she snatched her hair back. "I do not think we suit."

"We suited just fine when I made you come at the ball last night," he snapped. His nostrils flared and she caught her breath.

"I shouldn't have let that happen," she whispered, but she didn't feel it. She was glad he had done it, because once she had convinced him to go away, she was going to cling to that memory for all her life.

"Why did you say you didn't want to marry me?" he pressed. Now he moved forward, backing her against the door. He caught her hand in one smooth movement and surprised her by lifting it up and pressing it to the bell pull she refused to tug. As he leaned into her, letting her feel his heat, his hardness, he said, "Tell me, Mary. Or ring the damn bell."

Her hands were shaking as she stared up at him. She wanted to pull the cord. She *needed* to do it. But she didn't. And he smiled as he ducked his head and pressed his mouth to hers.

This kiss wasn't gentle like all the others had been. It was hard and heavy, filled with anger and desperation, and she dropped her hand away from the pull and wrapped her arms around his neck with a needy moan.

"You don't want me?" he growled as he pressed her harder. She felt the ridge of her arousal against her belly, and she gasped at how her body clenched in response.

"N-no," she lied, but she could hear how weak her refusal was.

"Then push me away," he taunted her. "Don't let me turn you..." He did so, maneuvering her away from the door. "Don't let me take you to your bed..." He backed her across the room, kneading her backside none too gently, making her gasp and shiver in response. Her legs hit the bed and she fell back, his body covering her.

"Don't let me claim you," he said, his mouth hovering over hers. "Push me away."

She lifted her hands to his shoulders, intent on doing just that. But as they rested there, as she stared up into his face, she couldn't find the strength, couldn't find the words. Not when she wanted him so very desperately. Not when she loved him so deeply.

"Please," she murmured as she clenched his shoulders.

"Push me away," he repeated, his tone rough and breathless.

She gasped out a sob. "I can't."

"I didn't think so," he murmured. Then he kissed her again.

There was purpose to the kiss. Drive that she couldn't deny. All she could do was open her mouth to him, open her body to him, surrender all her good intentions and her resistance.

He took them more than willingly, grinding against her as he took her lips. Her body responded to his roughness, arching toward him, her sex growing hot, wet, her nipples hardening beneath her thin nightgown.

"Now tell me you want me," he ordered her, pulling away from her lips to stare down at her.

She shook her head. "This is so unfair."

He arched a brow. "More unfair than sending me a letter telling me you don't want to marry me when you know we will be happy? When you know we both want this?"

"You don't understand," she pleaded, her eyes fluttering shut as he ground against her again and her sex throbbed in the most powerful way.

"And when I'm done claiming you, I intend to hear your explanation," he growled. "But first, tell me you want me."

"I want you, I want *this*," she whispered, going limp beneath him because she couldn't fight him anymore. Couldn't fight the truth. Couldn't fight her body's growing needs.

He rolled away from her just long enough to tug her nightgown up. She sat up and let him yank it away, leaving her naked before him. She blushed as he stared, but lifted her chin and forced herself to remain still beneath his scrutiny.

"By God, you are divine," he murmured. "Even better than I pictured. And I want you to look at me, Mary."

She did it even though it was hard to keep eye contact with him when he was so close, so hot, so distracting. "Yes?"

"I'm going to make you mine tonight. It will be like what happened at the ball last night, but with my body, not just my fingers. I don't want you to escape the future we have planned."

"Edward—" she began, intent on explanation, but he ignored the plea and cupped her sex, cutting off her words as he gently massaged the already sensitive flesh.

His fingers were magic, just as they had been the night before when he first gave her pleasure. Her words and thoughts and protests fell away, her mind and body only attuned to the sensations that began to mount in her.

He leaned over her as he continued to stroke his fingers over her sex, and suddenly his hot, wet mouth latched over her nipple. She squealed softly at the unexpected sensation and her sex rippled with the precursors of release.

"So responsive," he murmured before he swirled his tongue around her nipple. "And so sweet. Are you so sweet everywhere?"

She stared down at him at the question, not understanding it or why his words made her hips arch just a little more. He chuckled before he slid his mouth down her body, over her hip, and finally let his lips join his fingers at her center.

He traced her with his tongue and she jolted, eyes wide, at the intimate intrusion. He delved into the act, kissing her slit like he had so often kissed her lips. He held her steady with one hand while he breached her with two fingers of the opposite hand and licked her mercilessly through it all.

The pleasure mounted and suddenly, with little warning, starbursts exploded, her sex shuddered, pleasure won its war with anticipation, and she came. She turned her head into the pillow, letting her cries of release be buried in the fabric and feathers.

As the little tremors faded, he kissed his way back up the apex of her body, hesitating to swirl it around her nipples, to nuzzle her neck. Then he rose above her, positioning himself between her spread legs. He was still fully clothed to her nakedness and she lifted to rub against him, all propriety lost to pleasure.

"I won't let you go," he whispered. "Ever."

She watched as he pulled away, rising to his feet and slowly stripping away his clothing. She lifted to her elbows to enjoy the show of what he did. His jacket hit the floor, he loosened his cravat, then he unfastened his shirt to reveal a toned, muscular chest, peppered with a thin dusting of hair.

She swallowed hard, taken aback by a stunning urge to lick that handsome chest. But her thoughts were erased as he removed his boots and then his trousers.

As the fabric fell away, she got the first look at him fully naked, and she stopped breathing entirely. He was...*beautiful*. Like a statue carved of marble, the best representation of man. Only she didn't want to admire him from afar, she wanted to touch him. Tease him. Claim him and let him claim her.

She shouldn't, especially considering the danger he would be in once she did, but the temptation was overpowering. Her love for him and her desire to express it in this physical way was too great.

"Edward," she whispered. "Please. I don't want to hurt you."

He smiled as he returned to the bed, leaning over her, trapping her in a cage of his strong arms, positioning himself once more between her trembling thighs.

"The only way you'll hurt me is to deny me," he whispered as he stroked the hard head of his cock against her entrance. "But you won't, because your body has already told me that you want this, want me, want it all."

She squeezed her eyes shut. "I do want this. I can't deny you, even if I should."

He gently pushed and breached her just a fraction. She gasped, digging her nails into his shoulders with both pleasure and a hint of pain as he opened her untried body.

"You were meant for me, Mary," he continued, taking her a little more, just until he reached the barrier of her hymen. There he stopped and looked down at her. "And now you're mine."

He drove forward and she bit her lip at the rush of pain that greeted the action. But it was a good pain, one that woke her senses, one that made her feel alive in a way she had never experienced before.

He waited for her to relax around him and then slid further, further, until he was fully seated in her. She flexed around him, trying out his length, experiencing his girth. It was done now, over. She was his in the last and most powerful way.

So whatever was going to happen next, they would have to face it together.

With that terrifying thought in mind, she wound her arms around him and drew his mouth to hers. He kissed her with passion as he began to move, thrusting first gently. They were shallow movements that built the pleasure he had created earlier with his mouth. She surrendered to it all, meeting his thrusts, trusting him to give her what she needed, as much as what she wanted. And she was rewarded when he swiveled his hips, grinding against her clitoris, touching some equally sensitive place deep within her until she cried out into his shoulder as she came for the second time that night.

He groaned with her pleasure and his thrusts increased, harder and faster, pulling sensation from her, driving him toward his own release. She felt it coming, saw it on his strained face and finally, he let out a low, pained groan and she felt him pump inside her, hot seed soothing her, pleasuring her as he collapsed over her with a final satisfied moan.

Edward didn't know how long he lay with Mary in his arms, her tangled hair spread across his sweaty chest, her body curled into his. Time had ceased to have much meaning to him the moment he claimed her. But now, as the fire crackled and the moonlight shone upon her skin, reality began to return.

The reality of why he had come here.

He pushed her hair back so he could see her face and touched her chin, tilting it up to look into her green-gray eyes.

"There can be no secrets between us. Secrets will poison even the sweetest thing—I know this to be true," he said softly, watching her face light in fear, but also understanding. "Mary, why did you write me that letter? Why did you try to end our engagement? And please don't lie to me, because I will know it."

She blinked at tears that suddenly filled her eyes. Then she sat up, separating their bodies just as she had tried to separate their lives. She tugged her sheet up to cover her breasts and sighed.

"Your wife, she had twin sisters, didn't she?"

Edward tensed. Without even telling him the whole story, she had already given him all the information he needed. "Isadora and Imogen contacted you?"

"This afternoon." Her lips pinched together and he could see how ghastly it must have been for her. "They demanded I meet with them, and when I did, they threatened to destroy you if I went through with our marriage."

Edward shook his head. "Alice's sisters were defensive of her to a fault after her death. Funny, since the three of them despised each other before her suicide. But they are vicious bulldogs, the two of them. I can only imagine how awful they were to you."

Mary's nostrils flared. "Awful is not a strong enough word, I fear. They are monsters, and through them, I can see some of the monster your wife must have been." She reached out and touched his face. "I am so sorry, Edward. I wish I could take it all away."

"You do," he reassured her, and found that it was true. "Since you came into my life that sting, that horror has faded so much. But I need to know what they told you that frightened you enough that you decided your only course of action was to break our promises to each other."

She shut her eyes and a tear escaped one. "If I do not contact them by two o'clock tomorrow afternoon and tell them that our engagement is over, then they will go to the magistrate and tell him that they believe you...you *murdered* their sister. They will provide false stories that Alice feared you. They will say they came forward now out of a desire to protect *my* well-being."

Edward slumped back against her headboard, unable to hold himself up any longer.

"I always wondered if they would take their private attacks more public. I assumed their desire to protect themselves from the world finding out about Alice's suicide would stop them."

"And it has for a while," Mary said, her voice shaking like her hands. "But they hate you so much they do not wish to see you happy. They are willing to sacrifice a little of their own comfort in order to give you pain."

He nodded. "That sounds very familiar. After all, my wife threw herself down the stairs, willing to risk her own death, in order to punish me. Why wouldn't her sisters do the same or worse?"

"If they demand an investigation into Alice's death, it may go public. It *will* if they have any say. And there will always be people who believe you murdered her, even when they clear your name."

"If they clear it," he said, taking her hand. "Mary, you must know there is a risk I may be found guilty of murdering Alice."

"But you didn't!" she burst out, rising to her feet, taking the sheet with her.

"And if I had her journals or the letter she wrote before she threw herself down the stairs, perhaps I could prove that. But I don't."

She shook her head. "Why?"

"When Flynn was bashing himself into oblivion over Alice two years ago, your sister came to me and begged for my help to prove to him that she wasn't what he believed. Her love for him was so obvious, I couldn't refuse her and turned over the proof. She said she would destroy it all after he read both."

Mary's eyes went wide. "But she may not have. They may still have them. Come on!"

She rushed toward the door, and he got to his feet and grabbed her wrist just before she hurtled the barrier open and ran naked into the hall.

"Mary," he said, drawing her back. "You aren't dressed,

and if we come down together, looking as we do, they are going to know what we were up to."

She shook her head. "Good God, Edward, I was willing to end our engagement to shield you from their intentions. You don't think I would be willing to take a little embarrassment or wrath from Crispin?"

He pressed his lips together. "That is true. You were ready to face a life back under your father's thumb for me." He drew her near again. "Why?"

She stared up at him, lip trembling, face flushed. "Don't you know, Edward? I love you. And I would sacrifice myself, I would sacrifice anything, if it meant I could protect you."

He wrinkled his brow. Here in place of his bonny, winsome Mary was a warrior woman, clothed in a white sheet and the scent of their joining. She had fire in her eyes and a determination that made his heart swell.

"What did I do to deserve you?" he whispered.

She tilted her head. "You are just you. That is all I need or want."

"We will go down and speak to your sister and Flynn," he acquiesced. "But before we do, I must tell you, Mary, that you are the most splendid, unexpected and wondrous woman I have ever had the pleasure of meeting. And the fact that you love me as much as I love you, that is a gift."

Her eyes lit up. "You love me?"

He nodded. "With all my heart. Now, let us face this unseen future, shall we?"

She took his hand and lifted it to her chest. "Together. From now on."

CHAPTER ELEVEN

Mary should have expected the scene she found when she and Edward stepped into the parlor, but she still gasped and blushed. Crispin and Gemma sat together on the settee, curled in each other's arms, kissing. They were still fully clothed, but now that Mary had experienced passion for herself, she could guess that a few moments later and they just might not have been.

"Oh, excuse me," she said, turning her face as the couple broke apart.

Her sister stood up, her own face red. "Mary! We thought you were asleep."

"I couldn't."

Gemma had a strange expression on her face. Not that Mary could blame her. She had refused to do anything more but throw on her wrinkled nightgown and her robe to join Edward in his quest to find the proof that would save them from Imogen and Isadora.

Her sister's expression turned from one of confusion to shock as Edward stepped into the room behind her. His untucked shirt and untied cravat made what they had done together crystal clear.

A theory proven when Crispin jumped from the settee with a scowl. "What the hell are you doing here half dressed? What the *hell* is going on?"

Mary folded her arms, as ready to face Crispin's wrath as she had promised Edward she would a short time before. Knowing Edward loved her had only strengthened that resolve.

"Exactly what you *think* we have been doing," she snapped, ignoring Edward's groan behind her.

"You son of—" Crispin made to move on Edward, but Gemma caught his arm and tugged him back.

"Crispin, they are to be married," she said softly. "We have expected this could happen, and it does no damage."

"But to come down and flaunt this in our faces?" Crispin growled.

Mary sighed. "That is not what we were doing. I promise you, I would have greatly preferred to stay upstairs in my bedroom in the arms of the man I love. But something has happened and I need your help."

Gemma tilted her head. "Our help? What it is?"

She turned toward Edward. She could see he still hesitated about confessing their problem to Crispin. The two men had that shared history, after all. And they were not yet friends.

But Mary wasn't about to let such foolishness send her fiancé to the gallows.

"Please, Edward. Tell them," she said, taking his hand.

His jaw set and he nodded before he shifted his attention to Crispin. "Mary was asked to make a call on two old friends of ours, Flynn. Isadora and Imogen Brookfield."

Mary watched as both Gemma and Crispin paled. Her brother-in-law's nostrils flared as he clenched his hands. "The twin bitches." He looked at Mary. "They bothered you?"

She nodded. "They asked me to call on them and when I did, they threatened me. Threatened Edward, actually. If I do not break off the engagement, they will make a case that Edward...Edward murdered Alice."

Gemma lifted one hand to cover her lips, while she gripped Crispin's sleeve with the other. "Oh God."

Mary nodded. "I tried to do it, I tried to make Edward think I didn't want to marry him."

"What?" Gemma asked, moving toward her. "You said nothing."

Mary shrugged. "I was too brokenhearted. I couldn't discuss it tonight. I wrote Edward a letter and I went to bed and wished I would never wake up. I was going to tell you both tomorrow."

"But I refused to take no for an answer," Edward interjected as he took her hand. "By the by, thank you for planting that oak so close to Mary's window. Most obliging."

Crispin's jaw tightened. "So now what, they'll turn on you?"

Edward nodded. "That seems to be the gist of it. They will go to the office of the magister and try to get the whole incident reexamined, with an eye toward me being a murderer."

"But Edward says that two years ago, he gave a note and a journal written by Alice over to you, Gemma, for Crispin." She moved forward, pulling Edward with her. "Please tell me you still have them, for they may be enough to clear Edward's name."

Gemma shook her head. "They were destroyed."

"No," Crispin said, turning away from them all. "They weren't."

Gemma turned on him, her shock plain on her face. "What? You—you told me you would burn them."

He faced her, his expression drawn. "I didn't."

Mary could see how deeply that admission hurt her sister. Gemma went pale, her eyes filling with sudden tears. "Why did you keep her things?"

Crispin moved on her. "Not for the reason that is in your head, Gemma. *Not* because I still care for Alice, I assure you. I wanted to keep those things in order to remind myself that I was willing to throw everything away on a lie so I would never be so foolish again. I wanted to keep them as physical proof of how far you would go to love and protect me."

Gemma stared at him for a long, charged moment. "To the

ends of the earth, Crispin Flynn."

He smiled. "And back, I hope."

"Always back," she whispered.

Mary stepped forward. "So you have the items?"

"I do and I will gladly stand at your side and testify to everything that transpired," Crispin said, this time to Edward.

Mary could see her fiancé's shock at that offer. He shook his head. "You would help me?"

"Yes. For Mary, of course, but for more than that." Crispin sighed. "We were both hurt and deceived by Alice, you even more than I. And since you and I are going to soon be brothers, you should know that I protect my own."

Slowly, Crispin held out a hand, and for a long moment Edward just stared at it. Then he extended his own and the two men shook.

"That is a great ally, indeed," he said softly. "But rather than stir up this hornet's nest ahead of Imogen and Isadora with the officials, I have a different idea."

"Oh?" Gemma asked, smiling at the two men, even as she came to slip a comforting arm around Mary. "What is that?"

"I think we go into the lion's den itself." Edward squared his shoulders. "Tomorrow I say we pay a call to the Evil Twins and their grandmother, Mrs. Brookfield."

Crispin wrinkled his brow. "I don't think I ever met her."

"You're lucky. But unlike the twins, unlike Alice, Mrs. Brookfield has a bit more control over her vitriol. If we're lucky, we can play into her sensibilities."

"And if we're *not* lucky?" Mary asked, fear gripping her.

Edward looked at her. "Then we will go to war, my love. Together."

Edward had not been in the Brookfield family home since the day of Alice's funeral more than three years before. As he stood in the parlor, his hand in Mary's, with Gemma and Crispin standing behind them, he couldn't help but be mobbed with memories. Bad memories.

But then Mary squeezed his hand and the past evaporated almost like magic. He stared at her in wonder, and she smiled. "What is that look for?"

He shook his head. "You are a revelation."

"Standing here in a parlor with my heart pounding?" she asked.

"Standing at my side," he clarified. "I feel I could take on anything."

"Get ready to do just that," Crispin said, interlocking his arm with Gemma's. "I hear their so-called dulcet tones in the hall now."

Edward tensed. He, too, heard the harsh sounds of Imogen and Isadora in the hallway. Joined with them was the older but just as bitter voice of their grandmother and guardian, Mrs. Brookfield. As the door opened, he only barely resisted the urge to shove Mary behind himself, protect her from the venom surely to come.

Mrs. Brookfield had been in a wheelchair for five years and had worn full mourning black since the death of her husband twenty years before that. Despite this, she made a formidable figure as she stared up at him, spectacles perched on her nose and thin lips turned down in a frown.

"Lord Woodley," she said, his name like a curse on her lips. "I was surprised to receive your intent to call today."

"The nerve of him!" Imogen interrupted, coming forward with her eyes wild.

"Coming here with his whore fiancée and the bastard who defiled our sister?" Isadora joined in, glaring at Gemma and Crispin.

After so many years of keeping his calm in the face of their accusations and cruelties, Edward desperately wanted to snap back. But they had come up with a plan the night before and he was determined to stick to it.

"Mrs. Brookfield, may I present my fiancée, Miss Mary Quinn, and her sister and brother-in-law, Mr. and Mrs. Flynn."

A sniff was Mrs. Brookfield's reply. She motioned to one of the sisters and reluctantly Isadora moved behind her and rolled her grandmother to a space in the seating arrangement that had been left there for her chair.

"Why are you here?"

"Yesterday your granddaughters asked me here," Mary said, her voice strong and clear as she settled into a chair beside Edward's. Her sister and Crispin claimed another set and the twins took the settee closest to their grandmother.

At her words, Imogen shook her head. "No, we didn't."

"You did," Mary repeated firmly, giving the twins a dismissive glare before she returned her attention to Mrs. Brookfield. "They wished to blackmail me into breaking my engagement to Edward."

Mrs. Brookfield glared at her granddaughters. "Is this true?"

Isadora pointed at Imogen. "It was her idea."

"Liar, it was yours," Imogen burst out in response.

Mary took what appeared to be a cleansing breath. "I don't really care whose idea it was. My understanding is that your family hates Lord Woodley."

Mrs. Brookfield inclined her head. "We are not fond of Woodley, no."

Edward pressed his lips together hard before he said, "The feeling is mutual. And understood. But I cannot stand for blackmail, Mrs. Brookfield."

The older woman's smile was thin but bordered on triumphant, and Edward's heart sank. Was this trip for nothing?

"And what will you do about it?" Imogen asked with a side glance at her sister. She, too, looked unconcerned by his declaration. And why wouldn't she? As far as this family was concerned, they held all the cards.

Edward fought to retain control over his reaction to the

venom and the triumph when he spoke. "I believe your grandmother here would not initiate such a plan. It is too cheap for her, too little."

Isadora shook her head. "Careful, Woodley, or you will get to see what cheap and little can do."

Edward ignored her and held Mrs. Brookfield's stare. "Of course that doesn't mean you would stop them from carrying out their plan. After all, you like to cause chaos as much as the rest of them."

"Only to those who so richly deserve what is coming to them," the older woman said softly.

Mary gasped, but Edward merely nodded. "Exactly my point. Which is why even if I could convince these two vipers"—he motioned to the twins—"that they should leave me be today, I could never trust that you or they wouldn't take another opportunity to attack me another time."

Mrs. Brookfield's eyebrows lifted high on her forehead and Edward blinked. She actually seemed *interested* by this turn of events. Not angry, not upset, but truly engaged by the drama. Having raised Alice and the twins, he had often wondered how much their grandmother's treatment of them had been nothing more to her than a grand experiment. In pain. In disappointment. In turmoil.

"That is very true, Woodley," she finally said. "And just what do you intend to do about it?"

Across from Edward and Mary, Crispin dug into his inside pocket and withdrew the letter and the book that he had retrieved from his safe the night before. Gemma took them from him, her face a mask of disgust at having to touch them, and rose to her feet.

"What my wife now holds is the final journal that Alice was keeping at the time of her death. And the note written the night she died," Crispin explained. "I don't believe you ever saw these, although your granddaughters did."

Mrs. Brookfield snapped her harsh glare on the twins. "Did they?"

Both Imogen and Isadora flinched at the look. "You can't prove they are Alice's!" Isadora cried. Edward could see she was patently avoiding her grandmother's wrath-filled stare.

"You will find the hand and the signature are a perfect match to other writings that are known to be from Alice." Crispin pursed his lips, and Edward couldn't help but wonder if his friend was thinking of the lying letters he had received from Alice during the time she was using him. "No one would doubt their authenticity."

Mrs. Brookfield shook her head slowly. Her anger seemed to bubble beneath the surface, terrifying and far too quiet.

"They do not put your late granddaughter in a good light," Crispin said softy. "Gemma, will you hold the items while Mrs. Brookfield reads them?"

Gemma nodded, standing before Mrs. Brookfield as the lady leaned forward and read. The room was silent for a very long time as she reviewed both in detail. When she moved to touch them, though, Gemma stepped back.

"I'm afraid that I cannot allow," she said, and took her place with Crispin once again.

"If the contents of these items were to be revealed to the world at large, they would cause just as great a scandal as any accusation of murder you level against me," Edward said, once again taking charge of the exchange, though he felt the support of the others and it strengthened him.

"A scandal for you," Isadora said, but there was less certainty to her voice.

"Yes," he agreed. "Of course I would be swept up in the talk, as would all those I loved. But you would, too. You and your sister. Your grandmother. All your cousins. Everyone in your family would be sucked under in the wake of Alice's poison."

He watched with a smile as Imogen's eyes grew wide. She looked to her sister with a shake of her head. "Is that true?"

Isadora did not respond, but just swallowed hard. So it was finally sinking in.

"If you make a move to destroy me or my family, which includes the Flynns and those from the house of Woodley...I will take you down with me. *All* of you."

"How dare you?" Imogen said, but her grandmother raised a hand to cut her off.

"Do shut up, you two," she snapped. "It seems you have talked enough." The older woman leaned forward, examining Edward until his skin crawled. "So you have combatted blackmail with blackmail," she finally said.

He nodded. "I was left with little choice in the matter, wasn't I?"

"I suppose you were," she agreed, then shrugged. "Very well. You will have no more trouble from my granddaughters, I vow that it will be true. This is over between us."

She sent a glare to the twins, who folded their arms in unison, mirror images of rage, but also fear. They would be punished, Edward thought, for their keeping the journals from their grandmother, for the way they'd gone behind her back to hurt him. He shuddered to think about what that punishment would be. But he had more pressing matters to attend to.

"How can I be sure you are telling me the truth?" he pressed.

"You hold all the cards now. You have evidence that could hurt us. And I won't allow that." She smiled, but it was so ugly. "You know, Woodley, if Alice had just waited it out, I think you two would have been well-matched after all."

Edward swallowed back the bile that flooded his throat, but it was Mary who answered, "No. They would *not* have been. Come, I think we've lingered long enough. Good day."

She stood and the others followed her lead, walking out to the carriage and the fresh air. Gemma and Crispin got into the rig first, but as Mary moved to enter, Edward caught her arm.

"You set me free, Mary," he said in disbelief as he brushed a lock of hair off her cheek.

She shook her head with a smile. "We set each other free."

He leaned in and kissed her, right there in the open, right

there on the drive. And the love he felt for her swelled in him, bigger than the past, bigger than fear, bigger than the future that had once seemed so uncertain. With her it would be. With her, he could be nothing but happy.

EPILOGUE

Mary sidled up to her brand-new husband, drawing him away from the guests at their wedding breakfast with only a smile. Once they were away from the others, he looked down at her.

"Sneaking me off already?"

She laughed. "I would like to do so. First, I thought I should report that Audrey has crept out of the party. She looked a bit melancholy."

Edward frowned. "Did she?"

"Yes, perhaps you should go after her," Mary suggested.

He shook his head. "No, I will find Samson. He always had a better way with my sister than I did."

Mary nodded. Samson was her new husband's man of affairs. A tall, very handsome gentleman who clearly carried a torch that burned hot only for Audrey. But somehow she doubted her husband recognized that fact.

Honestly, she wasn't certain Audrey did, either.

"Well, if that will take care of one family drama," she said with a frown. "I will give you another. My father has disappeared. I fear he may be rifling your silver."

She laughed, but was only half-kidding. Her father had been boasting and hobnobbing all day. The fact he had now all but vanished was troubling.

"Your father left," Edward said, drawing her a bit further

from the crowd.

She tilted her head. "Left? Why would he do that when he can legitimately claim the attention of dozens of London's elite?" Edward cleared his throat and Mary tensed at the nervousness on his face. "What is it?" she asked.

He took he hand. "I know what he did to you, to your sister, over the years," he said softly. "And Crispin and I have been waiting for a very long time to put him in his place. Today we did so. Together."

Mary blinked. "I-I don't understand."

"Sir Oswald was promised a sum of money each month that should, if he can stay out of trouble, tide him over until the day he dies. Though perhaps not *quite* in the means to which he has grown accustomed. It was provided in equal parts by Flynn and by myself. To receive that money, he had to come to an understanding."

"Which—which was?" Mary whispered, hardly able to breathe.

"That he is not welcome in our home, nor in Gemma and Crispin's home, unless he is asked there by one of you. That he can expect no quarter when it comes to harassing or bothering you. The moment he does that, the *second* he violates that agreement, the money is gone and he will be shunned."

Her lips parted. "He accepted that?"

"Reluctantly." Edward's smile was thin. "I think both of us enjoyed how reluctantly a bit too much."

"So he will never...never bother me again?" She could hardly believe it. She had spent so many hours worrying over how her father would now insert himself into her happy life, how he would destroy her in new ways. But now she didn't have to fear that ever again.

"Never," Edward reassured her. "I will never allow it."

She wrapped her arms around his neck, the location and observers be damned. She held him close, shaking as she whispered, "Thank you, Edward. Thank you so much."

He leaned back to look into her face. "I would do anything

to make you happy, Mary. For the rest of your days."

"You do," she whispered in return, overwhelmed by the power of her feelings for him. "You do that and so much more."

Look for more books about The Wicked Woodleys—occasionally featuring the Flynn family—starting with Audrey's story, *Forbidden*, coming August 25!

SNEAK PEAK AT *FORBIDDEN*
The Wicked Woodleys Book 1

1816

Lady Audrey sat perched on the edge of the loft above the stable, dangling her stockinged feet through the hole that was meant for transportation of bales of hay and other equipment from below. She let out a sigh as she picked up the plate beside her abandoned slippers and took a small bite of her brother's wedding cake. It should have been a very happy day for her.

And it was. She was glad for Edward, her eldest brother who had been estranged from the family for three long years and was now coming back into the fold. She gave credit for that fact in great measure to his new bride, Mary. Audrey already knew they would be friends. Good friends, most likely.

But family gatherings always made her melancholy.

Audrey sighed as she took another bite of cake and stared out at the bright afternoon sky through the window across from her.

Below, there was sound of the stable door below sliding open and Audrey tensed as she looked down to see who had been sent to fetch her. Her tension fled when the person stepped into her view below her place in the loft.

It was Jude Samson rather than any of her three brothers or her mother. Jude, the longtime man of affairs for her brother, a man so much like family that all her brothers saw him as such.

And none of them ever noticed that Audrey couldn't stop...*watching* him. Even Jude was oblivious. He glanced up at her from below.

"Thought I'd find you here," he said, that rough voice swirling up between them and settling somewhere in her lower stomach.

"You know me so well."

She smiled down at him and he walked over to the ladder that led to the loft. He climbed up behind her. She forced herself not to look in his direction, but she felt him growing near regardless. When he set her discarded slippers aside and took a seat next to her, swinging his own booted feet through the hole to dangle next to hers, it was no surprise. She had guessed almost the exact moment he would do so.

She stared at their feet next to each other. It seemed very intimate, her stockinged foot just next to his booted one.

"Did you notice I was gone or did Edward or Mama send you?" Audrey asked, making herself look at his face instead of his boots. Some day she was going to do something to make him see what she felt inside. But not today.

He smiled and his rather stern face softened to a more gentle and youthful one. Hardly anyone else ever saw that side to him. Audrey knew that and recognized how special it was every time it happened.

"I *always* notice when you're gone," he reassured her.

She shook her head. "Oh, please, Samson. Don't try pretty words on me. Edward, then?"

Jude sighed. "And *you* always see through me, don't you? Yes, Edward asked me to come and check. But I did notice your absence, Audrey. I am not a liar."

"No, you are not that," she said softly.

They sat in silence for a moment, though Audrey wouldn't have necessarily said it was their normal, companionable type. Jude's smile was gone and there was something troubled in his eyes. Beautiful eyes the color of sapphires.

Damn, she really shouldn't wax poetic. Even in her mind. Jude was too bright not to notice and once he did everything would be ruined. It was bound to be, for he didn't care for her, not like that. Why would he? The man could have any woman he wanted. And if rumor was correct, he had.

The cloudy expression cleared before he spoke again. "Shouldn't you be inside celebrating Edward's marriage?"

Audrey shrugged.

Jude leaned away to examine her face. "Don't you like Mary?"

Now she jolted at his misunderstanding. Jude had been gone during Edward and Mary's odd courtship, so he seemed to still be uncertain of the new marchioness. Audrey didn't want to add to that hesitation.

"I do like Mary, very much," she reassured him. "You will too, Samson, I know you will once you get to know her better. She's really perfect for Edward."

He seemed unmoved by her declaration. He arched a brow. "But?"

She sighed. "But...but it is odd to welcome a new sister to our fold when Claire is still...*gone*. It's odd to all be gathered, except it isn't all of us. I look for her in the crowd, wishing I could talk to her about so many things, but she's just not there. And so I'm happy, but also, I'm..."

Samson nodded, looking away from her and down to the ground a floor below them. "I understand," he said softly. "Or at least I know what you're talking about. I doubt I could understand how much you miss your sister."

Audrey sighed. Claire had run away to be married to a most unfortunate man over a year before. Now she had all but vanished, taking her inheritance with her for the bastard to gobble up as he did God knew what to her.

But then, that sort of thing felt like it was the price of such passion. She'd seen it too many times in her family.

She set her half-empty plate aside and leaned back on the dusty floor with her palms. From the corner of her eye, she watched Jude. He looked guilty. But how could he be? He had searched long and hard for Claire, everyone knew how devoted he'd been to finding her.

"It isn't your fault, you know," she reassured him. "The only person she writes to is Gabriel, probably because they're twins. They've always had that odd connection. She never gives him an address so any of us could return the favor. Even the marks that indicate where the letters were posted changes every time a new missive arrives. She *wants* to stay gone."

Jude didn't look up. "It is still my job to bring her home."

"No, you're Edward's man of affairs, not his magician." She stood up and dusted off her gown. He joined her slowly, offering her a hand as she picked up her slippers.

"Here, balance on me," he said.

She smiled. "You do think of everything."

She rested one hand in his, ignoring the jolt of awareness that always came from that too-seldom action and used her other hand to pull her slipper back on. She repeated the action on the opposite foot and then released him.

"Ready to go back?" she asked, falsely bright. Nothing had been resolved, just as it never was. And although she could have stayed out here all afternoon, far into the night, with Jude, that just wasn't possible.

He nodded and motioned to the ladder. "You first?"

She swung over and climbed down carefully, then stepped aside to watch him do the same. It was quite the sight, really, observing Jude Samson's toned backside come down the ladder, see his broad shoulders strain as he moved.

She blinked and turned her face, forcing herself to stop. There was nothing good to come of desire. She knew that.

All she could do was try to squash the feelings that roared up whenever she was close to this man.

Other Books by Jess Michaels

THE NOTORIOUS FLYNNS

The Other Duke (Book 1)
The Scoundrel's Lover (Book 2)
The Widow Wager (Book 3)
No Gentleman for Georgina (Book 4)
A Marquis for Mary (Book 5)

THE LADIES BOOK OF PLEASURES

A Matter of Sin
A Moment of Passion
A Measure of Deceit

THE PLEASURE WARS SERIES

Taken By the Duke
Pleasuring The Lady
Beauty and the Earl
Beautiful Distraction

MISTRESS MATCHMAKER SERIES

An Introduction to Pleasure
For Desire Alone
Her Perfect Match

ALBRIGHT SISTERS SERIES

Everything Forbidden
Something Reckless
Taboo
Nothing Denied

Jess Michaels raffles a FREE Kindle or Amazon gift certificate EVERY month to members of her newsletter, so sign up on her website:
http://www.authorjessmichaels.com/join-the-jess-michaels-newsletter/

About the Author

USA Today Bestseller Jess Michaels writes erotic historical romance from her home in Tucson, AZ. She has three assistants: One cat that blocks the screen, one that is very judgmental and her husband who does all the heavy lifting. She has written over 50 books, enjoys long walks in the desert and once wrestled a bear over a piece of pie. One of these things is a lie.

Jess loves to hear from fans! So please feel free to contact her in any of the following ways (or carrier pigeon):
www.AuthorJessMichaels.com
PO Box 814, Cortaro, AZ 85652-0814

Email: Jess@AuthorJessMichaels.com
Twitter www.twitter.com/JessMichaelsbks
Facebook: www.facebook.com/JessMichaelsBks

Jess Michaels raffles a FREE Kindle or Amazon gift certificate EVERY month to members of her newsletter, so sign up on her website:
http://www.authorjessmichaels.com/join-the-jess-michaels-newsletter/